BEACH THING

DL WHITE

CONTENTS

———

"But...there's the other thing that's kind of important. And a few days ago, you said you had a hard time trusting women and not knowing their motivations. And that worrying about that is a distraction for you. I don't want to be a distraction."

"Ameenah—"

"And I don't need one, either. I might have made it here but I still have a lot of work to do to call myself a success down here."

"I get that. I'm not trying to be a distraction to you and if I am, I'll step back. But before I do, maybe we could just... have some fun."

"Have some fun?" Her eyebrows rose and her head cocked to the side.

"Not like you think I mean. I'm saying...we get along, we like each other. You impress the hell out of me, and that's saying a lot. I know I'm not going to be here long term but as long as I'm here, I'd really like to spend more time with you."

"And... have some fun." This time, her eyes were narrowed but her lips were bent into a smile. A small, sultry smile.

"And have some fun. A little beach thing, we could call it."

"A beach... thing."

Cover image courtesy *Deposit photos*

Cover by Dianne Frost- www.dianneinwriting.com

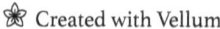 Created with Vellum

Ameenah

"A little more. More. *Higher*, Andrew!"

"Ameenah..."

Andrew grumbled, but lifted the sign higher. Perched on the top rung of the ladder, he held the long wooden board in place while my cousin secured it so it hung over the front entrance.

Once he had finished, we all stepped back to take in the view of the wooden building with the fresh coat of white paint and the *Tikis & Cream* sign finally hung. Satisfied, I smiled and let out a long sigh. It had been a long journey to *here*.

In the last six months I had upended my entire life to move to Black Diamond Isles, a cluster of man-made islands off the coast of Black Diamond Bay. I had found the perfect location for my coffee/smoothie/juice bar and renovated the space, doing a lot of the work myself to save money... and now I was *finally* open.

The *pièce de résistance* was a custom designed sign for the shop. My cousin, Liam, had shipped it from New York and he and my brother flew down to the island for a long weekend to hang it for me.

"Looks good, right?" Liam slung an arm over my shoulder, beaming with pride.

I stood in the middle of the sidewalk, just staring. I couldn't take my eyes off of the vibrant, beachy colors and the crisp lettering. My heartbeat sped up a little as I realized how it stood out amongst all the other shops on the boardwalk. I almost let a tear build up, but blinked it away. The long days and longer nights ahead would take care of that wistful feeling.

"It's beautiful," I told him. "I really love it. Now I'm official."

"You were always official, Meenah."

"Thanks, Liam. I mean it. For the sign, for coming down and helping me get things squared away. For... everything."

I hugged him, then stepped back to find my brother smirking, leaning his bulky frame against the counter. "You too, you big jealous fool." I gave Andrew a good heavy thump on the back, which he seemed to appreciate. "Even though all you did was hold the sign while Liam nailed it in, and stand around while he took care of my honey-do list."

"I paid for the tickets," quipped Andrew. "And I carried a couple of things from the house."

"He's a hard worker," said Liam, packing the last of the tools into a toolbox. "We'd better hit the road, though. There's an hour drive to the airport and if I miss my flight, the words Denise will use to describe me will peel the paint off of your walls."

I nodded, trying not to tear up again. This would be the last time I'd see them for a while. "I know she misses you and your help with the twins. Thank her for me, for letting you come."

"What about Kath? Should I thank her for you too?" I rolled my eyes, raising my arms to slide them around Andrew's shoulders. I squeezed him extra hard — our signature hug.

"Katherine has probably got so much done around the house without you."

"I love how you love me, Meenah." The jokey tone left his voice and his face took on a serious pallor. "You take care of yourself, alright? Don't hesitate to call, day or night. Well, not night because a man be working hard and be tired and everything..."

I giggled, appreciating the lightening of the mood before things got too heavy. "Thank you for everything you've done to support me. I know Mom and Dad think I'm crazy, but..."

I glanced back at the building, then up to my new sign, which marked the opening of my business. "This is my dream. Now go. As much as we joke, Kath will probably be happy to see you."

"Damn right," bellowed Andrew, picking up the backpack he'd toted to the shop earlier. "Man of the house comin' home!"

"He's all extra loud right now cause Kath would tell him to shut his big head up." Liam chuckled, then lifted his hand in a wave. "Ditto on what he said, though. Need us? Call us. We'll be here."

I watched them loaf down the sidewalk toward the main drag, where they would catch a cab to the small airstrip and head back to New York. Leaving me here.

In Black Diamond.

By myself.

A cold fear slithered down my spine. I shivered, trying to chase it away.

"Excuse me?"

I turned to find a middle-aged woman standing in front of my shop, holding a laminated half-sheet of paper— the *Tikis & Cream* menu. Her toasted cinnamon complexion bore a light sheen of sweat. "Are you open? I want one of these juice drinks."

I brightened, propping the door open. I flipped the CLOSED sign to OPEN, then stepped inside and behind the counter.

"Yes ma'am, I am open. What can I get for you?"

2

*W*ade

Gage grunted while lifting the case from the back of the moving van. "I mean, you didn't have to bring the whole studio."

"I didn't." I took the case from him, then shook my head. It wasn't even heavy. "You need to hit the gym."

"I hit the gym. I wasn't expecting a workout today. Is this the last of the stuff?" Gage peered around the open rear door, inspecting the now empty interior of the van.

"That's it. Everything is out of my car."

"Let's get this in the house, then. I'll show you where you can set up."

Gage grabbed a few items and trotted from the circular driveway into the house. I was a few paces behind, trying to get used to the fact that I would live in this... *house*, if you want to call it that, all summer. With six bedrooms, eight bathrooms, a heated pool and jacuzzi, three fireplaces, a fire pit and, just over the cliff, the white sands and blue waters of Black Diamond Bay, it felt more like a mansion, but Gage shrugged that off.

"Just a house, man," he'd said when he told me about his place on an island a few weeks ago.

We'd been in the studio all day, and it had been a rough time of it. Gage thought I needed a break and offered his beach place up for the summer. "We bought it as a tax break. I thought we'd be down there all the time but according to my wife, it's not better than her parent's place, so..."

He trailed off with a shrug, miscellaneously punching buttons on the console. "You're welcome to it. Sheree and the kids will still be in Jamaica."

It took me a few days before I felt comfortable accepting his offer, only relenting after he said he'd planned on driving down with me. "May as well get some use out of the place."

I stepped into the house, still feeling a little weird about the grandiose foyer and the expensive tile floors, the spacious rooms and the air of wealth that surrounded everything from the knick knacks to the fixtures. The fireplaces had gold plated pokers. I lived a simpler existence, so the excess tripped me out, but I was grateful to have a nice place to spend the summer. I could use the time and space away from the city. Away from the studio.

Away from my father, a man I never knew, had rarely seen except through a pane of glass and a telephone handset. A man who, a few weeks ago, popped up straight out of nowhere asking to be known. I *definitely* could use some time away from him.

"So I put everything in this room back here," Gage was saying as he rounded a corner. "I had extra power runs put in because that's where I was going to put my studio. There's a nice workspace near the windows so you get a view while you're working."

Half listening, I followed Gage to the back of the house. It *was* a nice area, more like an extended sunroom with a long span of windows along one wall. Beyond the pool and the extra acreage that surrounded the house, the Bay shimmered, washing up onto the sand. I kind of couldn't wait to set up on the beach in a chair with an ice cold beer, my iPod and some earbuds.

I exhaled, feeling the weight of the world lift a little.

"You alright, man?" I turned to find Gage studying me while flipping open the black cases that held the equipment he had driven down in the van. "I mean, this place is cool, right? You gonna be okay out here by yourself?"

"Oh, yeah. It's cool. It'll be a good summer."

I set down the cases and bags I was holding and joined Gage in getting the room set up. He'd be leaving the next day, so I wanted to take advantage of having two sets of hands.

Hours later, the room was starting to resemble *Tuneage,* my Brooklyn studio. I'd opened it after Gage's first release, produced by yours truly, jumped from the mid-20's to the top ten on the Billboard hip hop charts. We were a team, always had been since back in the day. Throughout junior high and high school, Gage wrote and rapped, sang a little, too. I was the beat factory and had a lot going on in my own right. The deal was that whoever hit it big first brought the other one along.

Gage was discovered on the radio, some New York morning show where wannabe rappers would call in and freestyle over a beat. He blew everyone away, and if that wasn't amazing enough, he got a phone call later that day that a major producer wanted to talk to him. Gage turned him down. "Already got Wade on the beats. He's the only one I work with."

After orchestrating a deal that included me, he released three chart topping records. His star was bright and while it should have gone to his head, it didn't. He was the same old Gage I always knew. Married his high school sweetheart, bought a nice spot, put his kids in Catholic private school. Gage Coleman lived a real good life.

I, on the other hand... I'm not saying my life was shitty, but I spent a lot of time at the Coleman's because I didn't have much of anyone else. My mother had worked long hours at a nursing home; my dad had been... *away* since I was young. We had no real family to speak of since my mother and her family were estranged after she got with my dad against their wishes.

Gage's family became my family, and it's always been that way. When he heard about my dad getting sprung and wanting to come around, Gage understood my freakout. But since his success hinged on me doing what I do, he wanted me to get it together, and *quickly*.

I wiped a few beads of sweat from my hairline and stood from a crouching position, where I'd been running some cords under a table. I took a glance around the room to see what else needed to be unpacked and plugged in, but things were looking nice. I still had to connect my speakers, run a few auxiliary cords, and take care of some minor things, but I figured that by the following night, music would be booming from this room.

I smiled at the prospect.

"You wanna grab some beers, some wings or something? The main drag is a few blocks away. We can walk."

I checked my watch. A feeling of emptiness in the pit of my stomach reminded me I hadn't eaten in a while. "Sounds good. I want to change my shirt. I'm covered in dust."

"You think you're gonna meet someone that cares about your dirty shirt?"

I laughed, heading to the bedroom I'd claimed for the summer. "You know your mama taught us to not look like just anything in public."

"I guess you're right. I'll change, too. You can't be looking better than me."

3

*A*meenah

I pulled down the metal shade to obscure the open counter, flipped the OPEN sign to CLOSED on the front of the shop and stepped outside, pulling the door shut behind me.

My first full day as owner and proprietor of *Tikis & Cream* was a success. I had a steady stream of customers, hot and sweaty from being on the beach and ready for a refreshing drink. I keyed both locks and checked the door, then weaved into the stream of foot traffic along the sidewalk. I was going to have to hire some help, sooner rather than later. If every day was like today—

A bump from behind me interrupted my train of thought. I turned to mutter an apology, but the words stuck in my throat. Two broad-shouldered men were so close, I caught a whiff of spicy cologne. I saw wide smiles on handsome, smooth milk chocolate faces bearing perfectly trimmed goatees. One had gorgeous amber-colored eyes, the other's were a deep, dark espresso and he seemed... really *familiar*. Both stepped aside as they passed me, nodding in my direction as they continued their conversation.

"Excuse you," I called out to muscle-bound backs. They turned to face me, genuine surprise in both sets of eyes.

"Excuse *us*?" said the shorter one. "You came out of there and didn't even look where you were going. I almost tripped over you. So excuse *you*, miss."

"You could have said something. You bumped into me, almost knocked me over—"

"Miss," said the taller one, lifting a hand, I guess to quiet me. "We didn't see that you were coming out of the shop. Excuse us. We cool?"

I huffed, folding my arms across my chest. "Fine. We *cool* or whatever."

He smiled and pointed two fingers at me. Then I recognized him.

I was letting my smart mouth run all over Billboard's number one hip hop artist, Gage Coleman! I had his latest release on heavy rotation on iTunes and my best friend, Paige, was madly in love with him.

My eyes grew wide and I sucked in a loud breath. He placed a finger over his lips and winked, then stuck out his hand. "Gage. This is Wade."

"I'm so rude. Don't mind me. Ameenah, nice to meet you."

Gage's grip was strong, his hand soft as I shook it. Wade reluctantly offered his, and I shook it, too. Now that I looked at him instead of glaring at him, I recognized him as Gage's longtime producer.

"We're looking for beer and good wings. Does that exist out here?"

"A couple of places, yeah. But if you're looking for something close..." I pointed toward worn out shack at the end of the block with the line out the front door. "Sparky's down there has great wings. Lots of flavors. Get extra napkins, though. They're messy."

Gage nodded, rubbing his palms together. "Good lookin' out." He eyed the shop behind me, then glanced at Wade, who rolled his eyes. "Looks like you're closed up for the day. Do you want to join us?"

I *wanted* to join them, actually. I really *really* wanted to hang out with famous, handsome men that had just happened to bump into me, but it had been a long day, I still had things to do before I could go to bed, I was tired as hell and my new job had disgraceful hours.

"Thanks, but I'd better be heading home. Maybe next time!" I walked around them, making myself leave before I did or said something stupid. Again. "Enjoy your wings!"

* * *

"Gage Coleman, in the flesh! And I recognized his producer, too. Wade something."

"Wade Marshall?"

Paige's voice rose to an octave I didn't think she could reach. "Are they as fine in real life as they are in this spread for MAXIMUM? Talking about Hip Hop's Dream Team. *Mmmmph*, Gage is *everything* I want on my team."

I laughed, dropping into one end of the couch with a bowl of ice cream. "I hope a bullet in your ass is something you want, too. Sheree Coleman don't play about her man. She will cut a bitch."

"Don't I know it. I heard about one girl in a club getting too close, kept hugging him, hanging on him, grinning all in his face and wouldn't step back. Sheree took right care of that mess." I heard her tongue clicking and pages turning. "Anyway, how long do you think they're in town?"

"I don't know. I haven't seen them before and I've been

here awhile. I'm guessing they just got here. And from the looks of the lights going on and off at the house on the corner, that's where they're staying."

"You mean that big house with the circular driveway and the pool and the... everything?"

"Mmmhmmm," I hummed, licking ice cream off of my spoon. I loved ice cream. It was my nightly treat — just a small bowl. To start with.

"How's everything going? You ready for me to come down there yet?"

"Actually," I said, almost choking on a too-big bite of chocolate chunk. "I'm going to need some help sooner than I thought. Not saying I can afford for you to quit your new job at that fancy law firm and move down here—"

"They won't miss me."

"Right. Does anyone else do any work? I'm sure you do everything over there."

"You're right. I am dope and they'd be lost without me." I rolled my eyes, even though she was agreeing with me. "So what are you going to do about getting some help?"

"See how long I can go before I fall over from exhaustion. Then probably place an ad in *The Bullhorn*." Black Diamond had its own newspaper for residents. If you needed to buy something, wanted to sell something, needed to announce something, it went into *The Bullhorn*.

"Please don't work yourself to the bone. At least not before I build up some vacation time and can come down there."

We chatted for a few minutes more while I scraped the bowl with my spoon — my signal that it was time to brush my teeth and crawl into bed. I set my alarm for 5:30 and I wasn't even sure that would be early enough.

"I'm turning into a pumpkin. Kiss everybody for me. Talk to you soon."

I signed off with Paige, dropped my bowl into the dishwasher and turned it on so it could work while I slept. A glint of light caught my eye as I passed the kitchen window overlooking the beach. I reached over to the wall and snapped off the overhead light, then waited for my eyes to adjust to the darkness.

I watched a figure trudge through the sand, just along the edge of the water, a mobile phone lighting up the night. Since he was walking from the direction of the house on the corner, I guessed that it was Wade.

Before I could stop myself, I opened the kitchen door and stepped out onto the deck, flipping on the porch light and walking to the edge. I leaned against the railing and waited for him to slip his phone into his pocket and make his way over.

"It's you," he said, when he got close enough for me to hear him.

"It's me, that loud mouth girl from earlier."

He chuckled. "I'm not saying all that. I was checking out the beach. I'm a city guy, so I don't get to see this often."

"This beach is great. I love the breeze off of the Bay at night." As if on cue, we both took a glance at the rolling waves, lit by the moon sitting high above. "So I guess we're neighbors."

He nodded, glancing toward the large house lit up like Christmas, then back to me. "It's Gage's place, but he's lending it out for the summer."

He paused, then the rest of the sentence rushed out of his mouth, like he was trying to beat me to some kind of finish line. "So listen, I'm sorry about earlier. I was tired and hungry."

I shrugged. "I was preoccupied. Should have watched where I was going."

"Well anyway, my mama raised me a gentleman. My apologies." He paused for a beat, then asked, "You run that little smoothie shop there?"

"I do." I nodded. "Just opened officially today."

"Yeah?" I heard the smile in his deep tenor. "No wonder you were preoccupied. That's good. I like to see people doing for themselves. Congrats."

"Thanks. You should stop by the shop tomorrow. I'll make you something on the house. If you want."

"You can't make money giving drinks away. I'll happily pay for something."

I laughed, stepping back from the railing surrounding the wood deck. "And I'll happily take your money. See you tomorrow."

4

----

*W*ade

"Say hey to the wife and the girls for me," I called to Gage's retreating back as he climbed the steps to board the aircraft. He lifted a hand to acknowledge me and then he was gone, swallowed up into the cavernous belly of the plane. Once the stairwell started to slowly pull up, I put the car in drive and pulled out of the private airstrip onto the main road.

Before long, I was crossing the bridge back into Black Diamond Isles. I was eager to park the car and then go find that little shake shack again.

And see Ameenah again.

We'd gotten off on the wrong foot a little. I felt like I fixed it last night, but patronizing her business would be a good move.

Not that I needed to be looking up women on the island already. Or at all. I had enough issues to deal with, enough things going on in my life that losing focus on a woman was just adding fuel to the fire.

She was pretty, though. The wild, deep brown curls that

framed her face were just barely contained in a clip. Her skin was golden, probably from working on the shop. Or maybe hanging out on her back deck. I noticed her thick lips when they were pursed and scowling in my direction. *And* I noticed those thick hips when she settled her hands on them in obvious displeasure.

I strolled the main drag between the beach and the beachside businesses. No vehicles were allowed on the street, only service carts, bicycles and foot traffic. I took my time, swinging my head from side to side, noting everything that was offered: t-shirts, beach swag, places to rent kayaks, canoes and stand up paddles, places to buy life jackets, water wings and snorkel gear. Then there were the restaurants — hot dogs, hamburgers, sausages, fries, wings, Italian ice and snow cones.

In the background, the Bay provided a regular, rhythmic soundtrack of waves rolling up onto the shore, then pulling back. I slept with my windows open last night, just to hear the sound.

I turned into the open door at *Tikis & Cream*, slipping off my shades and hooking them onto the collar of my shirt. The line was three people deep, so I stood to the side and occupied a high bar stool along the wall. Ameenah was pleasant and peppy, not showing a hint she'd been up too late investigating a creeper on the beach the night before.

Once her waiting customers had been served, she stepped around the counter, a wide smile beaming in my direction.

"You made it!"

"I had to make an airport run, see Gage off to join his family on vacation. I was checking out your menu. You think I could get one of these Frozen Sunshines you have listed here?" I pointed to an item on the menu, but she didn't need to look at it to know what it was.

"Coming right up. You want whipped cream on it?"

I shrugged. "Why not? I've already had wings and beer. My abs will be gone by the time I leave this place."

She laughed, moving behind the counter and deftly performing the tasks to make my drink. She had practiced a lot, it seemed. She knew where everything was without having to look for it, and everything she needed was in arm's reach. Whoever had designed her workspace knew what they were doing.

I had the same philosophy about the studio. No need for a huge space when I am going to use the same ten things over and over. May as well keep them near me.

"It's tempting to try *everything* when you're new to the island. Give yourself a week to explore; there really are some neat places here. And if you want, I can show you some healthier options. There's so much more to this place than the strip along the beach."

"Yeah, that'd be nice. There's a weight room in the house, but I'd like to get out every once in a while. Is there a gym nearby?"

She gestured for me to wait a moment, since the mixer was too loud to talk over. When she'd finished blending, she said, "There are two, actually. One tiny gym and one big gym, like Gold's."

"Sounds great. And like, the grocery store and a bank — which I'm sure I can find on my own, but if you're offering to be my tour guide..."

I took in the view of a bright orange, frothy concoction topped with a mound of whipped cream. "Damn! I might need to join that gym real soon if I'm going to be drinking these all summer."

"Now, this is made with fruit, ice cream and juice that have no sugar added, so I'm not giving you any unnecessary calories. Except for the whipped cream, but that's essential to finish it off."

She waited while I sucked some through the straw, then grinned at how fast my eyebrows lifted. "Yes?"

"So much yes," I swooned, sucking down more of the ice cold orange mix. "Very much yes. This is good."

"Thanks. I created it myself."

"Oh yeah? Well, you outdid yourself with this one."

She whipped a white towel from where it had been tucked into the back pocket of her khaki shorts, grabbed a bottle with a spray nozzle from behind the counter, and began wiping down surfaces.

"My family owns a restaurant group back in New York. One of the spots we own is a storefront near Long Beach. I worked a lot of summers there, and in the down time I would experiment with different combinations. I'm always trying something new with ice cream and fruit and juice... it's pretty interesting."

She'd been talking and wiping, making her way across the room. I'd been sipping and listening, watching her. Finding herself at the table next to mine, she set the spray bottle and the towel down and climbed up onto a stool. "At least... I think it's interesting."

"No, it is. It is. I mean, it's recipes, right? A little of this, a little of that, something to hold it together. I can relate."

"Yeah. A lot like that."

A small group piled into the shop, laughing and talking loudly, toting beach bags and towels. "That's my sign to get back to work. Let me know when you want that tour. Happy to do it."

I gave her a wave as I left, slurping the rest of my drink

and headed back to the house, set to get my room ready for work. I'd been off my game seriously since I'd heard from my father three months ago. It was coming out in everything I put my hands to. My work and my relationship with my mother were both strained. I couldn't afford to mess up either. Ruth Marshall was everything I had in the world. And without music, I may as well not exist.

As soon as I stepped into the house, my phone vibrated in my pocket. I pulled it out to glance at the display, but I already knew it would be her. Like always, exactly when my mind drifted to her, there she was on my phone. We had a crazy connection that way.

"Hey Ma," I greeted her, pressing the phone to my ear as I made my way through the house. I strolled through the kitchen and grabbed a bottle of water from the stash Gage had left in the refrigerator.

"So you're alive," she responded, dryly. Truth be told, it was her regular tone. She only perked up for company. "Good to hear your voice, son."

"Thanks, Ma. We made it yesterday, then had to get unpacked and everything before Gage flew back out this morning. Just now getting back to the house. What's going on up there?"

I listened to my mother give me a rundown of the boring things happening in Astoria. I'd offered to buy her a brownstone, something in Westchester or even out in the country upstate, but all she wanted was a nice place in the city she'd lived in for most of her life. She loved the upscale condo I bought her...updated interior, stainless steel appliances and the rooftop terrace. She and her girlfriends — The Biddies, they called themselves, liked to sit up there, drink and play cards with a view of Queens in every direction. Every once in a while she talked me into showing up so The Biddies could fawn over me.

"So you're really going to hide out on some island all summer, then? Leave your poor, destitute mother back in New York with no one to take care of her?"

I was laughing before she'd finished her sentence. I knew how much money I deposited into her account every month. She was nowhere near destitute, and she'd made friends with every resident in her building. I couldn't even stop by to take her to dinner nowadays. She was always rushing off to one thing or another.

"Stop, Ma. Don't make me feel guilty. You know I need this."

"Yeah." She heaved a deep, long sigh. I knew the feeling. "Yes, you sure do. Over the years, there were a lot of times I wished I could disappear. Have you heard from him?"

"I saw him a few days before I left town. I won't give him my number, so he doesn't call, but he found out where *Tuneage* is, so he'd been dropping by every few weeks."

I leaned my shoulder against the entryway to my temporary studio, watching the waves through the enormous windows. "I have nothing to say to him. You know?"

"Neither do I."

"Has he been in touch with you?" I pushed off of the wall and listened hard. If that man was bothering my mother I would be on the first thing smoking back to New York to let him know what was up. He'd been gone for a long time, far too long to mend broken fences.

"No, I haven't seen him since the last time I took you to visit him and you said you didn't want to go anymore. He stopped calling a bit after that. And then I moved and changed my number."

"Okay. Good. Let me know if you see him or hear from him. You hear me, Ma?"

"Don't worry, I will let you know. How's everything down in... where are you?"

"Black Diamond. You're welcome to come and check it out. Stay a few days. I'm right on the beach."

"Oh, you know I'm not really a beach person. It sounds nice though. Maybe later in the—" She paused at an electronic beep, then continued. "Hey, Neeta is calling me. She's supposed to come over and play Bid Whist. You take care of yourself, son."

"I will, Ma. Love you and say hey to Aunt Neet for me."

I slid the phone back into my pocket and headed to my studio, turned on some music, and got to work.

5

*A*meenah

    I heard music blaring from inside the house, so I wasn't sure if Wade could even hear the doorbell, but I kept trying it. He'd been coming by the shop every few days. I'd try to talk him into something new; he'd still choose the Frozen Sunshine, but promise that he'd try something new soon. I quickly learned that orange was his favorite flavor.

Which led to me standing at his front door with a plastic container of orange cranberry muffins, leaning on the doorbell like my life depended on it. I'd almost given up when I heard the music cut out. I pressed the doorbell button again, this time hearing it chime throughout the house.

I stepped back and waited for the footsteps that eventually came and for the door to swing open. The surprise on Wade's face as he opened the door made me giggle. That I knew of, he didn't know anyone else on Black Diamond — who else would be at his door?

"I've been standing out here so long, these muffins are probably cold."

He eyed the container and stepped aside to let me into

the house. "Sorry, I couldn't hear, with the music going. What's up?"

"Not too much. I just whipped these up for the shop." I gestured toward the container. "I thought I would bring you a few. They're orange cranberry."

The slow, sexy smile that spread across his face did things to my body, made it tingle in a way it hadn't in a while. I'd been so head down for the past few years, working two, sometimes three jobs to save enough to move to Black Diamond and open *Tikis & Cream*. I'd cut out dating and most forms of socializing. I only saw Paige when she dropped into the bar where I served drinks. I could catch my family at the weekly, non-negotiable Sunday dinner. Otherwise, unless I worked a shift with one of them, I rarely saw them.

Wade took the container and nodded his head for me to follow. I looked around while trailing him to the kitchen, my eyes wide at how the other half lived— Italian tile, dark marble, huge rooms with sweeping views. I thought I had a nice view of the beach from my little house, but the windows alone blew me away.

"So... Gage just lets you live in his house?"

"Yeah," he answered, pulling the lid off of the container and plucking a mini-muffin from inside. He grinned, then sniffed it, then popped the whole thing into his mouth. "Uhmm... *mmm*... these are good," he mumbled around a mouthful of muffin.

"Hey, don't choke. I'm not doing the Heimlich on you."

He chuckled, then reached for two more muffins. "These won't last the night. Guarantee. They're really good."

"Thank you," I said, feeling proud.

"Let me show you around. Gage and his wife don't really use the house as much as they thought they would. Her family has a spot down in Jamaica and she's used to going there. *Happy wife, happy life* is Gage's motto, so..."

He led me out of the kitchen, through a spacious dining room with a long cherry wood table and stately chairs covered in white fabric. We passed a formal sitting room and living room, ending up in what I supposed was the family room. It was much more casual and laid back — still upscale, but the room at least looked like it had been used.

"The house is here, sitting empty. I needed some time away from the city. Here I am."

He walked toward the patio doors and pushed them open, revealing a large wooden deck that put mine to shame. The sunset in the distance, only slightly obscured by clouds, gave us a gorgeous light show across the Bay.

He gestured toward a seat at the patio table, which had a colorful umbrella shading it, its panels flapping in the light breeze. "Can I get you something to drink? I can't make that orange thing, but I could grab you some water, juice or soda. Or I have some blood orange San Pellegrino, actually."

"I'm flattered that you would share your own orange concoction with me. I'll have one of those."

He left and returned with the container of muffins he'd left in the kitchen and two bottles of San Pellegrino. I took one and twisted it open, then gulped down a delicious swallow, tart and rich with orange flavor.

"Ooh, these are good. I might have to think of a reason to order them."

"You could create a drink with it. That would be amazing." He uncapped his bottle and practically poured half of it down his throat, then reached for another muffin. "These are all for me, right? Because I plan on eating all of them."

"Yes, Wade," I answered, laughing. "I was messing around in the kitchen, trying to create some things I could carry in the shop. I was thinking about your love for all things orange and remembered I had my grandmother's recipes. I made a few dozen, to try them out over the next few days."

"Well," he said, popping another one into his mouth. "These will be a hit."

"I'm so glad you like them." I paused, letting an awkward, too-flirtatious moment pass. "Uh...I heard music when I walked up. I hope I'm not cutting into your work time."

"Nah," he said, waving me off. "Don't worry about that. I'm always working, but you're never an interruption."

I blushed. Just a little. Obviously, two were playing this flirting game. "Noted."

"Especially if you're going to bring me treats."

He popped another muffin into his mouth and rubbed the palms of his hands together. "So, you said you just moved out here, but you know so much about the island. Is Black Diamond that small? You already made your rounds?"

"Oh, no. I used to come down here when I was a kid. My grandparents scrimped and saved to buy a little place to retire to. They're long gone, but I inherited the house when my grandmother died."

He turned his head to give a respectful gaze to the little red wooden house with the much smaller wooden deck. "That's nice. Real nice. Your folks are proud of you, I'm sure."

I almost laughed, but caught myself. "My folks think I'm out of my mind and making a huge mistake. We'll see, though. What about you? Have you already... made your rounds?"

He chuckled, weaving his fingers together. "I haven't

done much since I've been down here, but work. I probably need to take you up on that tour you offered."

"Probably," I said, nodding.

"Well... what are you doing tomorrow night?"

* * *

"So you're from Queens, but you live in Brooklyn now? What part?"

"The Heights."

Wade kept pace with me as we walked the streets of Black Diamond and I showed him the important sites — the bank, the farmer's market, the grocery store with the best prices and organic meat, both gyms, and my favorite bakery, Adele's.

Though it had changed hands over the years, it was still standing, still serving piping hot breads, pastries and muffins. My grandmother and I used to walk to Adele's on Sunday mornings to get half a dozen donuts, then sit on the deck and eat them. I still feel like she's with me when I splurge on one of the huge glazed pastries.

"That's... nice living," I commented. "Although it's bougie and upscale." I nudged him with my elbow.

"Yeah," he agreed with a grin, nodding. "It's a far cry from Queens, that's for sure. How about you? Where's your family?"

I almost didn't answer, because for all my teasing about Brooklyn Heights, my family's neighborhood was no slouch. "We're... uh... mostly around the Park Slope area."

Wade stopped in his tracks, tossed his head back and laughed. Loud and hard. "You talked about *me* being bougie and upscale? Ya'll live in one of, if not *the most*desirable neighborhoods in New York."

"Go ahead, tease away. My parents bought a place in the

70s and just... never left. When I was growing up, it wasn't like that. It was just home."

"I feel you. I don't really feel like Brooklyn Heights is any better than anywhere else. I've been there so long, it's just home to me."

"Gage is in Manhattan, right?"

He nodded his head, slurping down the last of the Frozen Sunshine I had made for him before we set out on our tour. He'd shown up just as I was closing up shop. I liked to be good and gone before the more rowdy evening beach crowd came through.

"Gage's girl is into nice things and nice places, and Sheree gets what Sheree wants. They have a nice spot, though. Very comfortable."

"Have you ever... I don't know, thought about settling down? Like them? Meet a nice girl from Brooklyn, have some kids?"

He shrugged a shoulder as his gaze swept to the side-walk. "Hasn't really been on my radar to tell the truth. My job takes a lot of commitment and it's hard when you do what I do."

"Hard as in how? Hard to open the door and see the women piled up outside of it?"

He laughed, dipping his head in mock humility. "I mean, I meet women all the time. Comes with the territory. But you can't just trust everyone you come into contact with. It's not like out here, where you just believe people are good, with honest intentions. You don't know people's motivations. Does she like me? Or does she like what I can do for her or get for her? Hard to tell."

"I guess I can understand that."

"Trying to figure it out is a distraction that I don't need. I date here and there, but I don't get serious enough to consider making room for her toothbrush, let alone for marriage."

I laughed at his quip, but also heard the gravity in his tone. I could identify with the sentiment, if not the situation. My family wasn't *overly* wealthy—we did alright, but I wouldn't say we were rich. But even I had side eyed a heavily interested man or two, especially after he learned that I was being groomed to take over the family business.

"Tell you what, though," he said, brightening. "Those muffins? These Frozen Sunshines?" He shook the empty plastic cup at me. "These are the way to a man's heart. Mine at least."

I chuckled, brushing off his comment and that tingle I'd felt the night before. I could *not* get my emotions tangled up with this man. He was on a plane much higher than mine.

And, I reminded myself, he was leaving at the end of the summer.

"So," I said, continuing my tour, "over that way is Brightman's. It's Black Diamond's oldest bookshop. They also sell stationery, some music, cool little knickknacks. Even if you're not a book person, you should drop in there at least once before you leave the island."

Wade nodded appreciatively. "Cool. I like to get my read on."

Against my better judgement and all my self-control, my heart bloomed. "Yeah? What do you like?"

"Horror, usually. King is the man. Koontz creeps me out, but I can't stop reading once I start. Gets my heart pumping. Lately I've been reading a lot of... what do they call it? Self improvement. Encouragement. I read Obama's books. Rich Dad, Poor Dad. Joel Osteen is preppy for me, but still a good word. Sometimes I just need a sentence or two to start my day off."

"I just started reading a book called *You Are a Badass*."

"Nuh uh." He glanced at me, then laughed when I nodded. "I'm going to need to borrow that when you're done with it."

"For sure. I'm almost done. I'll bring to the shop and you can grab it the next time you're in."

"Or... you could bring it by the house and let me treat you to dinner."

I opened my mouth to quickly decline, but the words wouldn't come out. I couldn't tell if he was flirting or being nice. Not that it mattered... did I really have time to be spending with this man?

On the other hand... I knew he was leaving at the end of the summer. He knew he was leaving at the end of the summer. He wouldn't try to start something knowing he'd have to walk away from it?

Would he?

Thinking back to our conversation about settling down, though...

"I see you over there, trying to figure out how to let me down gently." He grinned, showing off a perfect smile.

"I'm... not. Actually." *What the hell am I doing?* "When you say treat me to dinner..."

"Exactly what I said. Now that I know where to buy good food, I want to go grocery shopping, light up that big ass stove in that big ass kitchen."

"You cook?" *Jesus, help me.* "What can you cook? Like what's a dish you cook well?"

"You ask like you're expecting me to serve Pop-tarts and Spaghetti-o's. Don't worry about it. Just come by on Saturday. Around seven. Is that enough time to close up the shop and get home?"

"Plenty. I'm looking forward to Pop-tarts and Spaghetti-o's."

We continued walking, picking up the path that led to the strip along the beach where we'd begun our journey.

"And if you show up without those little orange cranberry things, I'm not letting you in the door."

*W*ade

 I didn't know what I was doing, to be honest. For reasons unbeknownst to me, because I had no desire or intention of starting something up with Ameenah, I set out to impress her with my culinary skills.

I spent the morning at the grocery store, the afternoon cleaning and cooking. I *should* have spent the day working, but I'd opened my big mouth and let an invitation to dinner fall out of it, so I had work to do.

By the time the doorbell rang, dinner was ready and so was I. My one-pot pasta with spinach and tomatoes alongside marinated, grilled chicken breast filled the house with a scent so good, it made *my* mouth water.

"Door's open!" I called out into the foyer from the kitchen. My hands were in oven mitts and I was getting ready to pull the butter and garlic crusted Texas Toast out of the oven.

For a whole three or four seconds, I forgot what I'd been about to to do. Ameenah stepped into the house in a sleeveless white dress that showed off long, tanned legs and pretty toes in sandals. Her hair was pulled up and piled on top of her head so her curls framed her face.

Her very pretty face with those thick lips that I'd been thinking about way too much, lately. Like how soft they must be. And what she'd do if I tried to kiss her.

She held a bright yellow book in one hand. And in the other was another one of those containers I liked.

"Am I overdressed?"

"Oh..." I glanced down at myself in dark jeans and a shirt I'd wear to go golfing. I cursed myself, thinking I should have put more thought into what I'd put on. "No. No, not at all. You look nice. Come on in, my bread is burning."

She followed me into the kitchen and settled onto one of the stools that lined the counter. I pulled the bread out of the oven and transferred it to a serving dish. Then I stirred up the pasta and started transferring it into a dish.

"Smells really good in here. I haven't eaten since lunch."

"You're in for a treat, then. This is one of my mom's favorite dishes that I make."

"Oh, it passes your mother's taste test?"

"Hell yeah. She's the one who taught me how to make it. *Ain't no sense in putting it on the table if it's not gon' taste good, son. Just wasting your time. Do it right.*"

She giggled at my imitation of Ma. "My mother likes my coffee drinks. Daddy saves his calories for bourbon."

"My *man*. Maker's Mark?"

"One of his favorite brands, yes."

"Be nice to have a drink with your old man. Hear all about Park Slope before it was... how did you put it? Bougie and upscale."

"Get your jabs in now... he's fiercely protective of his neighborhood."

I grabbed two serving platters and gestured for her to grab the third. "You don't mind eating on the deck, do you?"

We settled in and served ourselves, chatting over pasta and fork-tender slices of chicken breast, then had after-dinner drinks while we exchanged stories of growing up in New York — me in Queens, her in Brooklyn.

"You ever live anywhere else? I mean, not just in New York, but the world?"

We had moved inside and away from the mosquitos that seemed to feast on her calves. We settled close together on the love seat in the family room with our drinks and the container of muffins she'd brought.

"I lived about six months in Virginia Beach. We recorded Gage's second album out there. He was in and out. I got a place down there and just stayed in the studio. Mixing, coming up with beats, new sounds. He likes to bring something new to every project, and I'm with that."

"It seems to be a philosophy that's paid off. Who wants to buy an album that sounds exactly like the last album you put out?"

"Right. We don't do part two of anything. Whole new vibe. Whole new sound. I spent a couple of weeks in Hawaii, some time in South Beach, but other than touring, we don't travel away from home too much. Everything we need is right where we can get to it. Designed that way."

"Must be comforting to not have to look too far, to go searching."

"In some ways, yes. But the status quo has a way of lowering expectations. I can't do great things in the same old surroundings. I need something new to disrupt the usual, to inspire me."

"Thus, your temporary move to Black Diamond."

I nodded, suddenly feeling like I had talked a lot,

opened myself up a lot to this woman I barely knew. "What about you? Why uproot yourself and move so far away from your family and everything?"

She reached down to her calf, subconsciously scratching at a mosquito bite. "Like I said, I came down here a lot when I was a kid. I was close to my grandmother and after she died, we never came back here. I just... really missed the place.

"I've always worked for my family, with my family. I was supposed to take over Porter Hospitality, co-run it with my brother. When grandmother passed, she left me her house and her shares in the family restaurant group. I really felt like she was telling me something, you know? I just wanted to be close to her, I guess. And I wanted to branch out and do my own thing. Build my dream, not my parent's dream."

"That's dope. I mean, it probably took years to get here, right?"

"She left me the shares ten years ago. I've spent the last five years pulling together what I thought I would need to get set up here."

"I really admire that, Ameenah." She blushed and waved me off, but I grabbed her hand and held it, letting my thumb sweep over her soft skin. "That's hard work. Dedication. Laser focus on your vision. And now you're here. And I don't know if you're worried or not, but... don't be. You're already past the hard part."

She didn't respond for a few moments, and I was worried that I'd offended her. Her gaze was fixed on my hand enveloping hers, on my thumb moving side to side, back and forth. It was hypnotic to me, but I had no idea what was going through her head.

"Wade..." she finally whispered, her voice a little ragged from the two Amaretto sours she'd had. "I'm... I don't know what's happening right now. And I don't know if I should fight it or let it happen. And I don't even know if you know what I'm talking about."

"I know." I gripped her hand and scooted closer, dropping the other arm around her shoulder. "I know exactly what you're talking about. And... I don't know what's happening either, but even if I could fight this, I don't want to."

"I... I just... you know, you—"

"I'm only here for the summer. And I'm some big important famous guy that lives in fuckin' Brooklyn Heights. And I like orange flavored things. Right?"

She huffed a laugh, those pretty brown eyes rolling hard. "Okay, it's that last part. It's not that you're only here for a short time. It's not that you live in some expensive neighborhood." She leveled her gaze at me and batted her eyelashes. "It's your unnatural obsession with orange flavored things."

"I feel like that's something we can work out."

"Yeah. But...there's the other thing that's kind of important. And a few days ago, you said you had a hard time trusting women and not knowing their motivation. And that wondering about that is a distraction for you. I don't want to be a distraction."

"Ameenah—"

"And I don't need one, either. I might have made it here, but I still have a lot of work to do to call myself a success down here. I have a lot to prove to myself and to my family. I risked a lot to move here."

"I get that. I'm not trying to be a distraction to you, and if I am, I'll step back. But before I do, maybe we could just... have some fun."

"Have some fun?" Her eyebrows rose and her head cocked to the side.

"Not like you think I mean. I'm saying...we get along, we like each other. You impress the hell out of me, and that's saying a lot. I'm not going to be here long term but... as long as I am here, I'd like to spend more time with you."

"And... have some fun." This time, her eyes were narrowed, but her lips were bent into a smile. A small, sultry smile.

"And have some fun. A little beach thing. When the summer's up....so are we. But in the meantime..."

"A beach... thing." Her bottom lip crept between her teeth.

"Hold up," I said, gripping her chin and tipping her head up. "Let me take care of biting that lip for you."

She released her lip and sucked in a quick breath before my mouth met hers in a soft kiss. I pulled back a little to find her eyes still closed, and I wasn't all that sure she was breathing. I dipped back again to get another taste of her lips, this time letting my tongue glide along the seam until she opened her mouth. With a moan, I played with her tongue, nibbled at her bottom lip, all while keeping the kiss light and airy.

"Whew," she said, huffing a breath, placing a hand over her heart, which I hoped was racing. "I uh... wow."

"Thanks for all of that. Makes a man feel good to know he can take your breath away."

She laughed, then reached for the last watery mouthful of her drink. She sucked it down and settled back into the couch, almost imperceptibly moving closer to me. Almost.

"That kiss was amazing. And I'm not just saying that because I haven't been kissed since before Obama's second term." I laughed, but she eyed me. "I'm serious. I mean, a peck here and there, but men today don't know how to kiss."

"You're saying I know how to kiss?"

She nodded, vigorously. "I'm saying you know how to kiss. Which makes me wonder..."

"I know how to do that too. Did you need a demonstration?"

"Actually..." She inhaled, then exhaled a deep breath. "I am so flattered. And a little drunk. And... I need to go home before I do something stupid. Can I think about... the beach thing for a bit?"

"I would be okay with you doing something stupid... but I'm cool with you taking your time. No matter what you decide, I'm still going to come by for my Frozen Sunshines. And I better see some muffins now and then."

She cackled, and I felt her mood and uneasiness lift considerably. I hoped it was enough to eventually tide her over.

And if not? I didn't need to be dating, anyway. I was *supposed* to be distraction-free.

I walked her back to her house and waited at the front door for her to get her keys out. I gave her a hug, during which she squeezed me extra tight. And then... I couldn't help it. I lowered my head and caught her lips in a kiss that she didn't protest. Her hands slid up my chest and her arms drew around my neck.

We must have kissed for a good five minutes before she pulled back, blinking and breathing hard. "I... need to go inside," she said, her voice so airy and sexy.

The whole evening had been doing things to my body but this last blow with the way her voice sounded told me I would be spending some time in a cold shower when I got back to the house.

I stepped back when she unlocked the door and swung it open. "Hey, sleep good, Ameenah. I'll see you tomorrow."

*a*meenah

The last customer of my daily lunch rush walked out of the shop, already slurping down his blueberry and green tea smoothie. Wade passed him on the way in, his eyes on the lavender tinted beverage in the plastic cup.

"Was that guy drinking something purple?"

"Blueberries do that to a drink."

He approached the counter, then leaned over it drop a kiss on my lips. "Hey."

"Hey," I whispered, biting my bottom lip. I did *not* want to be this silly, awestruck girl but... he just made me so giggly and swoony. I made myself sick the way I'd tossed and turned the night before, reliving every second of the evening from the time I walked in the house until he kissed me at the door.

"Can I get my usual? And uh...."

He stepped back to peruse the selection of muffins and breads that I'd put out for the day. "Shark Bites," he said, pointing to the sign hung above the baskets. "Cute. Would these Danish things happen to be orange flavored?"

"They would be. You're very perceptive." I grabbed a napkin and selected the best looking one, then set it on a paper plate and turned to make his drink.

"You spoil me, that's all that is." He took his pastry and headed to his regular seat against the wall.

"How was spin class?"

"Oh, it's *SoulCycle*. I spoke to Roderick this morning and made the mistake of telling him how much I was enjoying his *spin classes*. I think half my ass is missing."

The blender whirred, spinning the orange, ice cream, and juice into a frothy substance. I poured it into a cup, then grabbed my can of whipped cream and topped it off with a flourish. I finished it with a straw, then walked around the edge of the front counter to deliver it to his table.

"I don't believe I just burned a ton of calories and then I came here to eat them back." Then he slid the rest of the pastry into his mouth and brushed the crumbs from his fingers. "Oh well. They taste good coming back on."

"How are those abs doing?"

As if by reflex, he lifted his shirt, showing off a chest covered in a fine layer of hair, molded pecs and a very... *defined* set of abdominals. As in, brother had more than a six-pack going on and shouldn't have to worry... *ever*... about his abs. A breath hitched at the back of my throat and I almost choked on my tongue. I reached out to touch him, but I heard a customer enter the shop behind me. *Fuck!*

I snatched my hand back, and he dropped his shirt, then stuck the straw in his mouth like he'd done nothing wrong. I playfully scowled at him and mouthed, "don't move," before I turned around to help the next customer.

Wade wandered the shop with his hands in his pockets while I helped the next customer. And then the next. *And the next.* I apologized with my eyes — it seemed I was getting another rush and business came first. He shrugged, mouthed that he would see me later, and ducked out of the shop.

* * *

I had wiped down tables, swept and mopped the floor and was emptying the garbage when Wade strolled through the door, as casually as if it hadn't been hours since he walked out. He slipped off his shades and, without a word, grabbed the garbage can from my hands, pulling the bag out and tying the ends in a knot.

"Where does this go?"

"There's a dumpster back there, behind the building. But you don't have to—"

"Be right back," he said, carrying the bag out of the door like it only weighed four pounds. I pulled down the metal shade, grabbed my bag and my bank deposit, and pulled the door shut. I was locking the door when Wade came back around the building.

"Thank you for doing that. It wasn't necessary, but thank you."

"I like to make myself useful. So... what are you doing right now?"

"Bank run. Then heading home. You?"

"Going with you to the bank. And then home."

"Home? Like... my home?"

He shrugged. I laughed, then stepped in close to him, tipping my lips up to his. He gave me the sweetest, softest kiss. If I was being honest, I had been thinking about him kissing me all day and I was expecting a little more. When I angled up to him again, he pulled back.

"I just emptied garbage. It's gross back there. And I'm

still sweaty from my workout. I'd like to get somewhere I can wash my hands before we get uh... started."

"Fine," I whined, rolling my eyes, grabbing him by the crook of his arm and pulling him with me down the sidewalk.

A short time later, Wade had my propane grill smoking with seasoned chicken on one side and vegetables roasting on the other. I was at the bar, being imaginative with what I had on hand.

"Okay, try this." I handed him a mason jar full of ice and a fruity cocktail.

He took it and sipped. Then sipped again. "Bourbon. And... orange. Hm." He took another sip, then licked his lips. "That right there is a hit, baby."

"Yeah?" I beamed, impressed with myself. "You like it? You're not just saying it because I'm pretty and you're hoping to sleep with me?"

He choked on his next sip and had to cough it out. "I'm not just saying it. Although..." He coughed, then took another sip from the mason jar. "You are beautiful. And no pressure, but I am very much hoping to sleep with you."

He bent toward me, and I knew he meant for it to be light and sweet, but it had been almost a full day since he'd kissed me and I was obsessed with him doing it again. I hooked my arm around his neck landed a long, strong kiss on his lips. He picked up the hint and tipped his head, opening his mouth.

The taste of bourbon and orange, coupled with the sensation of his tongue swirling with mine, heightened all of my senses. I rose up onto my toes and sank into him, feeling very much protected by the muscular arms that drew around me.

"Mmmmm," he hummed when the kiss ended. "That was nice."

"I thought so. You taste good."

"Does that kiss mean what I think it means?"

I shrugged, pulling back. I tried to get away, but he hooked a thick arm around my waist. "Ameenah—"

"Wade, the chicken is probably—"

"Fuck the chicken," he said, grinning. "So... Beach Thing?"

I tipped my head side to side and tried to stop smiling. It was impossible. I had no idea what the fuck I was doing... but some cobwebs were about to be swept out.

"Beach Thing," I finally answered.

Wade gave me the widest, sexiest smile I think I have ever seen. "Beach Thing!" he bellowed, then leaned in to kiss me.

"But seriously, the chicken—"

"Oh." He whipped around, tongs in hand, ready to turn the seared breasts.

* * *

"We make a good team," I said with a sigh as I collapsed onto the couch. Dinner had been devoured and drinks enjoyed in view of the setting sun over the Bay. I couldn't have asked for a more romantic setting if I tried. Before the mosquitos started feasting again, Wade suggested we move inside.

"You mean me on the grill, you on the drinks?"

"Exactly," I mumbled, my eyelids halfway open.

"I guess we make a good team in that regard." He glanced over at me, sprawled unladylike across the couch. "Hey. You're not falling asleep on me, are you?"

"Hmm-mmm. I'm up."

"I'm not convinced, Ameenah. You have to be tired. You've been up since... when?"

"Five am. But I'm up," I muttered, from behind closed eyes. "You know what I need?"

"Uh..." He snickered. "Yeah, actually, I do."

One eye opened. "Besides that. Some ice cream. I eat ice cream every night. That's where these glorious hips come from."

"Oh yeah?" I felt him move across the couch, settling beside me so he could lean over and kiss me. One hand gripped my side and slid down my body from hip to knee and back up. "I happen to like these glorious hips."

My other eye opened at the sensation of him touching me. "You do? After all those twiggy chicks that must hang all over you?'

"Nothing against thin women at all, really. But uh..." His hand coursed my body again, this time creeping up under my t-shirt on the way back up. I felt the pad of his thumb slowly rub across my nipple, which sent a volt of electricity through me. "I do really... *really* like the hips. I like everything, actually."

"Been a long time since I met a man that liked everything."

He laughed. "What does that mean?"

"Oh, you know. *I'm a boob guy, Ameenah. Or I'm an ass man. Or I like feet. Will you show me your feet? I don't care about nothin' else, just the feet.*"

My imitation of the last three men I'd gone out on dates with had Wade laughing hard. "That's crazy. How do you not just... feel like a body part?"

"That's why they ain't get none. But you like everything. And why you're about to get it all."

His eyebrows shot up, and his jaw dropped open. "I'm about to get it all?"

"If you want it," I whispered.

He nodded, suddenly serious. "Hell yeah, I want it."

I sat up, swinging my legs to the floor and drew him to me, taking him by surprise when my other hand sought and gripped a thick, warm muscle through his shorts.

"Ay! I mean... *ayyyy*..."

He leaned into me, resting his forehead on mine. I massaged him, catching his eye and holding his gaze. His eyes were half open, and glossy, either from the bourbon or... me.

I hoped it was me.

My fingers flitted to the button closure on his waistband and popped it open, then pulled the zipper down as slowly as I could handle it. Considering I wanted to rip his shorts off, I commended myself for my self-control.

Wade reached behind his neck to pull his t-shirt over his head. "There are those abs again." I smiled, reaching out to run the tips of my fingers down and then up the well-formed muscle.

"I'm sucking in my Frozen Sunshine gut," he said, laughing. It died down quickly when I pulled the band of his boxer shorts away from his body and dipped my hand into the opening. He was erect, like his dick was just waiting to be unwrapped. I closed a palm around him and swiped my thumb across the head.

He throbbed. And moaned. And licked his lips. "What are you doing to me, Meenah?"

"Isn't it obvious?" I smiled up at him, squeezing him gently. "Seizing the dick."

I could tell by his smile and quiet laughter that he was amused, but he was way more interested in my hand action.

He chewed on his bottom lip as I danced my fingers down his shaft, then up one side and back down again.

"That feels good," he mumbled into my ear, between nibbles. Then he cradled my head in one of his big hands, holding me close while he kissed me and I stroked him, pulling and twisting. Under my t-shirt, his thumb alternately circled my nipples, then flicked the tips through the flimsy lace fabric of my bra. The shocks that rolled through my body made me moan and squeal, even though my tongue was heavily occupied.

Sooner than I wanted him to, Wade brought his head up and pulled my hand out of his shorts.

"You're not trying to cut me off, are you?"

"Nope." He pushed himself up from the couch and reached for my hand to help me up. "Just hoping we can get a little more comfortable."

I led him down the hall to the largest of the two bedrooms. I flipped the wall switch, which turned on the bedside lamps and lit the spacious room in a soft glow.

He made a full turn, taking in every nuance of the space from the vintage curtains sewn by my grandmother to the restored knobby wood pine floors covered by handwoven rugs. "Wow. I like this room. It's so... *authentic*. That must be great in the winter," he said, pointing to the fireplace.

"It cools down just enough to use the fireplace. It's cozy."

"Mmm hm." He gripped my hips and pulled me close, up against him. "I know what else is cozy."

"Oh. Can I take a guess?"

"Yeah. But I'm going to show you, anyway."

Wade moved, sliding his shorts and boxers from his hips while shuffling us backward until the backs of my knees hit the mattress. I pulled my t-shirt and shorts off and climbed up onto the bed in bra and panties, scooting back against the pillows.

He followed, pulling me down and then rolling on top of me. He growled, his mouth claiming mine, his hips gyrating and my hips matching him thrust for thrust.

"Wade..."

He stopped, angling to catch my eye. "You need to stop?"

"No... I just don't want you think I'm looking for candlelit romance and slow dancing or anything. I'm ready. I've *been* ready."

"You *been* ready, huh?" Wade grinned, showing off that sexy smile that sent tingles to every edge of my body. "What happened to, *'Wade, I just need to think about it....'* Huh?"

I giggled. "I was drunk. And horny."

"So now you're just horny. And seizing dick."

I shrugged. "Carpe dickem, as my friend Paige would say."

"If you don't mind, I want to check out that 'ready' situation myself."

I answered by opening my legs wider and pushing his shoulders down. "By all means, Mr. Marshall... don't let me stop you."

Wade scooted down in the bed, all the while emitting the cutest, but most evil-sounding snicker. He nipped at the inside of one thigh and then the other, working his way toward the center.

He hooked his fingers into the waistband of my panties and pulled at them until I lifted my legs so he could pull them off. "Stay right there," he said, holding my legs up in the air and tossing the thin fabric to the side... then burying his face in my pussy.

At the first flick of his tongue on my clit, I clenched. "Oh, shit!"

"Relax," he said, his lips so close to me they brushed my clit. Then I felt his lips on me, licking and sucking, almost to the rhythm of my repeated grunts of "*yes, yes, oh my God, yes*" and "*Holy shit, I'm about to come!*"

"Nuh uh. Not yet." He released my legs, which felt like lead. Or Jell-O. They fell wide open, in perfect position. Wade sat up and reached for his shorts on the floor. "Do not move. I mean it. Don't move."

"You expect me to follow your directions when you don't follow mine?"

"What? What do you mean?"

"Earlier today. I told you not to move. You left."

"I had to go—"

I laughed. "I *really* wanted to experience those abs up close and personal. You took them away."

"I had to go home and get these." He pulled two square foil packages out of his pocket and tossed the shorts aside. "Now you're about to experience everything up close and personal."

"Everything?"

Wade climbed back onto the bed, ripped one of the condom packages open and rolled it on. He maneuvered himself into prime position between my legs, gripping the underside of a thigh with one hand, and balancing himself with the other.

"Everything," he confirmed, sliding into me with a firm but gentle thrust. "Just relax. I won't hurt you."

"Oh, my... *fuck*." I was full... so full... the fullest I had ever been. It felt... so fucking good. "I'm not... *unnnfff*... worried about you hurting me."

"So you say. You aight?"

"Hmmm," I hummed, nodding vigorously. Deliriously. "I'm... so good. Oh, my God. Keep going."

"Okay. Let me know if—"

"Wade! Shut up and fuck me!"

I laughed, mostly out of delirium, then cupped his chin with both hands and brought his face to mine. I kissed him, sucking on his tongue in long, languid strokes in a rhythm I hoped he would pick up.

I opened my legs wider and rested my arms across his shoulders. His head dipped to my neck, where his hot breath puffed against my skin. He varied his strokes from a pounding *thrustthrustthrust* to a sensuous grinding against my clit, then changing it up again.

"*Unnhhhh.... fuck!*" He moaned, softly at first, then louder. "Wade, baby? You comin'?"

"About to." He panted, lifting his head. He wiped a sheen of sweat from his brow. "Waiting on you."

"You go, I go. Come for me."

His thrusts became longer, harder, joined by deep, guttural grunts. I hunched my hips so he rubbed against my clit with every stroke. I felt him pulse, then release a long, loud groan as he plunged deep into me.

"Holy...*shhhhhhhhh*—" The rest of the word was swallowed up by a massive, body pulsing climax. My hair stood on end and the room went dark for a few seconds. Wade pumped in and out and didn't stop until I grabbed his face and kissed him.

"Okay! Okay, okay, okay... before I pass out."

He chuckled, gripping the condom and pulling out. "Just making sure the dick was seized."

I heaved, sucking in air, trying to catch my breath. "Oh. That dick was seized." I swallowed thick, sex scented air and then grinned like a fool. "Carpe'd. All of that."

8

*W*ade

"I don't think I've ever celebrated great sex with ice cream before."

She grinned, scraping the sides of the small wooden bowl. Her nightly ice cream ritual was a prelude to sleep, so we'd sat in the middle of the bed and shared a bowl of Ben and Jerry's Raspberry Fudge Chunk.

"Got to live a little, Wade. Enjoy life's pleasures."

"Didn't I just enjoy one of life's pleasures?" I leaned over to nuzzle her bare shoulder with my cold lips. She squealed and leaned away, setting the bowl on the nightstand.

"You want me to take that into the kitchen for you?"

"Nope. I want you to kiss me."

I leaned in, brushing my lips across hers, then sucking her bottom lip into my mouth before sweeping my tongue against hers. I couldn't get enough of her soft lips, the taste of her mouth, the sounds she made when I kissed her, like it was the most pleasurable moment of her day.

"You taste good."

"Mmm." She smiled, coming in again for more. "So do you."

"So, I don't want to crowd your space or anything. I know you need to get up early. Do you want me to go?"

The look on her face at the suggestion that I leave reminded me of the look my mother used to give me when she thought I was giving her nonsense answers. I was fine with leaving... if she wanted me to go. But I was looking forward to sleeping next to her, feeling her body heat next to mine. Well, for real, feeling her *body* next to mine.

Which, to be honest, was a rare want. I liked for the women I slept with to get it on and then get out. I didn't like to share my bed, my home... my life. But Ameenah was different.

"You can stay if you want to. Unless you're just aching to go home. I'll understand." She heaved a dramatic sigh. My lips did away with that.

"Nah. But would you have an extra toothbrush? Bourbon and ice cream will have my breath kicking you in the face in the morning."

She let out a cute little snort, rolling out of the bed and heading toward the ensuite bathroom. "I'm pretty sure I have a brand new brush. I'm gonna take your hint about the breath."

"I... I wasn't saying.... I just..."

She tipped her head out of the bathroom, smiling. "I was going to grab a shower. You're welcome to join me."

I rolled off of my side of the bed and in three steps was crowding her in the small bathroom.

* * *

The good food, the bourbon, the sex and the ice cream all had me knocked out until Ameenah shook me awake the next morning. She hadn't turned the lights on in the bedroom, so through the one eye that crept open I could only see her in silhouette, with the light of near sunrise through the window behind her.

"It's almost six," she whispered. "I'm about to head to the shop, but I left you some muffins, and I made coffee. Make yourself at home."

"Unh," I grunted, trying to come to, but the cloak of sleep was heavy and her bed was comfortable, like sleeping in a bed at the Four Seasons or the Ritz. "I gotta...go to Soul-Cycle anyway..." I yawned and stretched and fought against rolling over and going back to sleep.

She chuckled, then leaned over me to kiss my temple. "See you later for your usual?"

I sat up halfway, leaning on one elbow, cupped her chin and brought her face to mine for a proper kiss before she left.

I heard the front door close and the crunch of her footsteps in the mix of rock and sand down her driveway. When I finally felt somewhat awake, I forced myself out of the bed... and laughed. Ameenah had made the bed on her side cocooning me in. All I had to do was pull the sheets tight, adjust the pillows and fix the comforter and the bed was made.

I bent to pick up the shorts I had discarded the night before, but they weren't on the floor anymore. I looked around for them, finding a small pile of folded clothes stacked on a chair next to a bookcase. I bent to peruse the titles she had collected.

There were a lot of books on building businesses, accounting for the small business owner and some of the inspirational and educational variety. The bottom shelf was full of romance, which didn't really surprise me. I could imagine her sitting in that chair, daydreaming and reading with a view of the Bay just outside the window.

I swept my clothes from the chair and heard a heavy thunk as something fell to the floor. I picked up my phone and clicked the button to wake it up. I'd put it on silent when I left the house the day before. The only person that could break through was my mother, but we'd already talked and I didn't expect to hear from her.

So seeing that she had sent me a text made my heart skip a beat. I hadn't heard it because I'd left it in the living room.

Ma: He came by here earlier.

Just those five words made my lip curl. My bum ass father was bothering my mother now, probably trying to get in touch with me. I didn't have a number for him, so I couldn't call him and let him know what was up. I checked the time — it was past 7AM. Ma was an early riser, usually up with the sun, reading the paper and drinking tea.

I quickly pulled on my shorts and brought the rest of the pile out to the kitchen. A small pot of brewed coffee sat on the kitchen counter, the red light glowing to let me know it was still warm. A burnt orange mug had been placed next to it, along with a tray of muffins and a note: *'Cream in the refrigerator, sugar in the metal tin next to the coffeemaker'.* She'd signed it with a smiley face.

I scrolled to a familiar number in my VIP list and put the phone on speaker. While it rang, I emptied the carafe of coffee into the mug and turned the pot off.

"Mornin', son." She sounded more chipper than usual, which lightened my mood some. It told me she wasn't bothered about seeing Ruben. At least, she wasn't showing it. "Isn't it a little early for you to be up? The whole point of vacation is to relax."

"It's past seven. And I'm not on vacation. I'm here to work. I have my cycling class this morning, anyway."

"I guess it's good that you're getting out, not sleeping your life away on the beach. How are you?"

"I'm okay. I saw your text this morning. How are *you*?"

"Oh, I'm fine. I don't need you to do anything. I just wanted you to know he was here."

"Did he say anything to you? Did he come to your actual apartment or just to the building? How does he even know where you live?"

Ma laughed, making a choking sound. "So many questions. Can I get a word in?"

"I don't want him bothering you and I want you to stay safe."

"It's not like he's dangerous. He didn't kill nobody."

"Nah, he just stood around and watched shit happen and went to prison for it. I went my whole life without a dad because he was supposed to get a third of the come-up and he ended up the one getting caught."

"You've got to let some of this anger go, Wade. It's useless to you."

"*He's* useless to me! He wouldn't even name the dudes he was with on some honor shit. How about some honor to your woman? To your son?"

"Wade Anthony." The tone in her voice, one I knew well, and the use of my middle name told me to back up and fix my attitude.

I inhaled deeply and ran a hand over my uncombed hair. "I'm sorry, Ma. I don't mean to take it out on you. I wasn't even thinking about him until he showed up a few months ago. Now he's over at your place trying to get to me."

"I just want you to check yourself, because Ruben

Marshall is not worth worrying over. He's not worth the emotion. Let it go."

"I..." I was about to say I couldn't, but Ma wasn't going to be into that answer at all. "I'll try. So how did he get in the building and how can I make sure that doesn't happen again?"

"It's already taken care of. I told you I didn't need you to do anything, and I meant it. He buzzed someone and asked for me, and they let him in. The whole building knows now to not let anyone in asking for me. Anyone who needs to be here already has a code."

"Okay. Okay." I was breathing a little easier, knowing she was relatively safe. "As long as you're alright, Ma."

"I'm fine. Now go get your day started with your... cycling classes and whatever. I'm going to be late for stitch & bitch."

I chuckled. "Aight, Ma. Say hey to the Biddies. Love you."

I slid the phone into the pocket of my shorts and finished fixing my coffee. I grabbed the mug and the plate of muffins and slid open the patio door. The sun was up, a bright orange ball rising in a cloudless sky. It was turning out to be a nice day already.

I sat on Ameenah's patio, drank coffee and ate muffins and watched the waves roll in and out. In my mind, thoughts about Ruben rolled around — his insistence on trying to contact me, his efforts to build a relationship with me after all this time. I wanted no parts of knowing him, let alone spending time with him, letting him into my circle, trusting him.

His son's name was on some records. His son had made the Billboard charts. His son was well known in producing circles. His son was a big deal. And now that he was out of prison, he could play on that. I was sure he was already telling people that he was my father, trying to take credit for a talent that he played no part in cultivating.

All that time he was in prison, it was Ma paying for records and equipment. It was Ma lending me money for studio time. It was Ma encouraging me, giving me leads, spreading the word if I was spinning in a club or doing a local show.

It was Ma and Gage and the Coleman's and everybody *but him* at the first album release party, nodding heads to *my* beats, smiling at how I transitioned from one vibe to another.

Ruben Marshall didn't have shit to do with that. But now he wanted to come around and claim his son and try to "help". Nah. There was nothing Ruben could do for me.

And there was nothing I'd be willing to do for him.

I finished up my breakfast and cleaned up my mess before I left, pulling the door shut behind me. I double checked that it was locked, then trotted down the stairs toward the house. I already knew my cycle class was going to be spent working out some emotions surrounding Ruben. I was looking forward to it.

Beyond that, I was looking forward to seeing Ameenah after class.

* * *

"What's a guy gotta do to get some orange flavored drank?"

Loud and obnoxious on purpose, I strolled into *Tikis & Cream* to find Ameenah alone, with her trusty spray bottle and white towel, wiping down tables. Her lunch rush had already gone, since I was showing up later than usual.

"Hey!" Her big, pretty smile made my day better just on its own, but then she put down the spray bottle and walked over to me and planted those lips on mine. "I thought you might have gotten caught up with work."

I grabbed her up in a hug, landing a kiss near her ear. "I took Rodney's hip hop step class after SoulCycle."

"Look at you, getting into the workouts!"

"I had some things I needed to work through and it helps me think. Something I need to look at keeping up when I get home. I have a weight room at the house and I do videos here and there, but it's nice to get out and take a class live."

"I kind of miss it," she said, wiping down the last table and tossing the bottle and the towel into a basket behind the counter. "I've been thinking about advertising for help. I can't keep working seven days a week."

"And staying up 'til all hours of the night with your Beach Thing."

She wiggled her brows at me. "Speaking of Beach Thing... do you want your usual?"

I started to nod, but thought better of it. "Tell you what. I trust you — you know what I like. Whip me up something new."

It was cute and funny and sweet how that suggestion excited her. She clapped her hands together and took inventory of all of her juices and mixes, pacing one end of the shop to the other.

"Okay, I think I'm going to have to go rogue. Do it on the fly. Stand back."

A few minutes later I held a blend of mango, banana, orange juice, yogurt and ice, served in a plastic glass with a sugared rim and a cherry. The taste was amazing, and the ice made it cool and refreshing.

"I like this," I said, barely taking time away from sucking it down to comment. "I like it a lot. Kinda sweet, but not. The yogurt gives it a nice texture."

"I've been working on something like it for a while, trying to come up with a signature drink for one of the spots my family owns."

"I'd say you're well on your way to something memorable. A little rum or some bourbon would make it a nice cocktail."

"Hmmmmm. I'll have to think about that— what I could mix with it to give it a different taste." Musing, she stepped behind the counter to clean up the blender. "So, I need to ask you something."

My eyebrows lifted, but my mouth was still occupied by the straw in my drink, so I just grunted.

"Uh, so... my birthday is next week. I'd planned on closing the shop and doing something fun on the water — maybe take stand up paddle lessons? I thought maybe if I let you work and not disturb you for a few days that you could take the day off and spend it with me."

I choked on my quiet laughter, setting the cup down. "I already told you, you're not an interruption. And if you think you can live two houses down and me not see you for a couple of days when we only have a short time together, you're way wrong."

"Oh." Her lips remained frozen in the 'O' shape for a few beats. "But... you *are* supposed to be working and I don't want to be—"

I glared at her— playfully so but she got the point. In small bursts, I was getting a lot done. I'd sent some samples to Gage, and he was wild about them, asking for the full track so he could start writing against them.

I reached for her, pulling her from behind the counter and sliding my arms around her waist. She fit into me, up against me like a glove. She smiled up at me with that innocent, *Who, me?* expression.

"What did I just say, Ameenah? Seriously, what did I just say a minute ago?"

"That I'm not a distraction. And that I'm crazy if I think I won't see you for a couple of days."

"Okay, then. That's how it is. As a matter of fact, I'm working a lot more here than I was at home. Getting a lot done." I bent to kiss her, a light brush of my lips against hers. "Don't worry about me. Aight?"

"Fine. I won't, then. So next Wednesday?"

"I'll work it out. But you're really closing the shop for the day? That's right before the holiday. Every shop around here is gearing up for the flood of people they're expecting. You want to miss out on that kind of money?"

Ameenah lifted a shoulder in a shrug. "I've always taken my birthday off. It's my favorite day; I'm not going to spend it working. I want to hire and get some help trained between now and then. But if not, the shop will be closed."

She rose onto her toes and kissed me. When she pulled back, she was grinning. "Don't worry about me. Aight?"

I laughed, hearing my words come back at me. "Fine," I said, parroting her. "I won't then."

meenah

"Oooold maannn riverrrr."

"Oh, Lord."

"Oooold maannn riverrrr."

Wade crooned in a smooth and freakishly deep voice as he floated past me on a paddleboard, stroking easily through the calm water. Neither of us had ever tried stand up paddling before, but Wade took to it like a fish out of water.

I, on the other hand, was having a harder time of it. "I keep feeling like I'm falling over."

Wade glanced over at me, then directed his paddle board toward me. "Because you are. You're not balanced. Remember, the guy said both of your feet should be in the middle of the board."

"My feet are where they were when they got on this thing and I'm not moving."

"Come on, Meenah. This was your idea—"

"I didn't think it would be this hard! How hard can it be

to stand on a — whoa shit!" The board tipped heavily, nearly flipping over with me on it.

"Okay, hang on. Just stand still." Wade maneuvered himself next to me, then grabbed my arm above the elbow. "I've got you. You're not going anywhere. You need to move those little feet, or you're gonna flip yourself."

With him holding my arm, I felt a little more stable. Or at least like he wouldn't let me fall overboard, not that it would matter since I wore a swimsuit under shorts and a tank top and he wore trunks. I mostly didn't want to deal with the embarrassment of falling into the water.

I inched my feet to the center of the board and planted myself as the instructor had shown us earlier that morning. Then I gripped the paddle and dipped it into the water, pulling like I was in a kayak instead of standing on a thin wooden board I'd rented for the day. It sliced through the water like butter and my board followed the current, moving forward.

"There you go," said Wade, still holding on to me. "Let me know when you feel comfortable enough that I can let go."

"Uh... not yet." I took another stroke and moved again.

"Stand up straight. Keep your feet planted. There you go. Good girl."

The longer I paddled, the more comfortable I felt, until I told Wade he could let go. When he did, I felt an almost immediate surge of panic, then tamped it down. I stood up straight, planted my feet and cut through the water again. In a few minutes I was comfortable enough to make longer, stronger strokes.

I pulled up alongside Wade, who had been lingering and circling while I got comfortable.

"You good?"

"Am now." I smiled over at him. "I thought I had it this morning during the lesson, but being out here without the instructor is..."

"Different?" He squinted into the sun, then pulled his shades down from their perch on top of his head.

"Yeah. But I'm good now." We floated peacefully, keeping an easy rhythm alongside each other. "So, you have a nice voice on you."

"Yeah," he said, but didn't elaborate.

"No interest in singing?"

"Nah," he answered, fixing his gaze on the tip of his board.

"Hmmmm. Okay."

He paused, looking back at me since he had just passed me. He looked... irritated. "*Hmmm, okay* what?"

"Nothing. I... guess you don't want to talk about it. It's cool."

He reversed his stroke and moved backward, then brought his paddle out of the water. "My voice is about the only thing I got from my dad. Besides my face. And honestly... I don't want shit from him."

My questions weren't timid but weren't bold, either. More like softly lobbed. "So you don't know him? Or... want to know him, then?"

"I know who he is. I've seen him, more than I want to, lately. We don't have a relationship. He's just a guy that has nothing to do with the man I am today. So maybe we look alike and I can sing a little bit, but..." He shook his head, his expression solemn. "I don't want that from him."

"Understood. I didn't mean to bring up a difficult subject."

"You didn't." He brightened, nodding his head toward an inlet where we had planned to stop for lunch. "You asked me about my voice. I'm the one that made it weird. So, sorry about that."

We paddled over to where the land jutted out a bit from the shore. Now that it was the height of midday, it was a good time and place to stop. We pushed our boards up onto land and laid the oars next to them.

I opened my backpack and started setting out our lunch — deli sandwiches, fresh fried kettle chips, pickles and orange cream cake with granola crust. Bottles of water and blood orange San Pellegrino were buried deep in the bottom of the bag, staying cool under ice packs.

"How come on your birthday, I'm getting the treat?" He dug his fork into an individual serving of cake and shoveled a scoop into his mouth.

I laughed, scraping the sides of the plastic container. "You're with me, doing something I want to do. Can't help it if you're enjoying yourself."

"Guess I'm lucky we like the same things."

"Or we're willing to try the same things. You never got on a paddleboard before today?"

"Nope." He shook his head, licking his fork clean, then tossing it and the container into the bag I'd brought to cart our trash back with us. "City boy. Just good on my feet. I always wanted to try surfing, but as many times as Gage and I have been to Hawaii, we've never found the time to get out there."

"That all work, no play thing is serious, I see."

"We play." He smiled, coy and mischievous. "Gage is probably out on a boat with his wife right now. I'm playing with you right now."

"That you are." I started piling up wrappers and containers to put inside the bag. "Wade... I wanted to apologize. You said it wasn't a big deal, but I can hear it in your voice that talking about your dad bothers you. I guess I was just being nosy. My dad and I aren't as close as we used to be, but I can't imagine not having him."

"Yeah? What's up with Mr. Maker's Mark?"

I shrugged. "I told you that my family owns Porter Hospitality, right?" He nodded. "Well, ever since... forever, I've known that the plan was for me and Anthony— my brother — to take over for them. Breaking the news that I wanted to sell my shares and move to Gran's house on Black Diamond was... well, let's just say it wasn't well received. My parents felt they'd worked hard to build a company their children could take over. When Gran died, leaving the house and her shares to me, the assumption was that I'd sell the house and put that money into the company.

"And for a long time I was with the plan... until I came down to prep the house for sale. Just everything about this place — the house, the sand, the breeze. Brightman's and Adele's and all the little shacks that have been around here since I was a kid..."

I sighed and glanced up at him with a wistful smile. "I was so overwhelmed by my memories. I felt... I had a longing to be here, stronger than anything I'd ever felt before. I felt like I was supposed to live out some kind of legacy. Gran left all kinds of things for me, things that reminded me of my childhood summers with her. I couldn't let it go."

"And your parents don't get that." Wade watched me while sipping from his bottle of San Pellegrino.

I shook my head, slowly. "And I guess that's why I didn't tell them. Which was wrong. They could have had all of that time to get used to the idea, but I was scared. So I plotted behind their backs. I made some repairs, had some renovations done, but kept my secret to actually occupy the house."

"So nobody knew what you were doing?"

"Paige knew from the beginning. I called her from Gran's house in tears and hysterics. I couldn't sell that house. I needed to be here. She'd come down with me every few trips to help renovate and update. But what we were really doing was planning how I could do this.

"And eventually, Andrew knew. He'd been running three restaurants already. My parents said they thought I was ready to take over the other three, and I fell apart. I showed up on his doorstep in tears and then sobbed through my disappointment at my "promotion". We came up with a plan for me to do what I wanted to do."

I paused for a beat, awash in emotion. I'd packed a lot of it away, since I'd arrived on the island. I was *here*... no sense in crying about it. But Mama and Daddy had called exactly once, since I made it to the island, to see how things were going.

"Seems like this should be a time for being proud of their daughter. But... maybe parents get blindsided by what they want for you. It was probably hard for them to let go."

"Yeah. Probably." I reluctantly agreed to his point. "Anyway... as much as my folks and I aren't getting along I really can't imagine not knowing them or wanting to know them. But I guess I've always had them, so..." I lifted a shoulder in an apologetic shrug. "I just wanted to say I was sorry for being nosy."

"I'm really not bothered by your curiosity, or whatever. Your questions are innocent, because you don't know him and the history that's there with him. Other people though... people that think they know me and know the best for me—"

He paused, drawing his lips inward. I reached out, landing a hand on his forearm. His head whipped around to me as if he'd forgotten I was there.

"It's okay, Wade. You don't have to... it's okay."

He gave me a look that I read as appreciation for not pushing more. Then he leaned over and pressed a sweet kiss to my lips. "Lunch was good. Even though it was *your* birthday and I should have brought lunch for *you*."

"You can make it up to me later, Beach Thing."

Wade laughed, the mood finally lifting a little. He uncrossed his legs and stood, reaching out a hand to help me up.

"Let's get back on this water. We can talk about later... later." He wiggled his brows at me before he turned to pick up his paddle and push his board back into the water.

* * *

After a full day on the water, plus lunch and a short session of making out in the middle of the Bay, we turned in our rentals and headed toward home.

"I kind of want to drop by the shop," I said, hiking my backpack over my shoulder.

"Why? You want to spy on your employee?"

I shrugged. "I just want to make sure everything is going okay."

"She made my Frozen Sunshine just how I like it yesterday, so I'd say she's doing okay."

Dionne, my new employee, was a riot to work with — bright and energetic and took to the running the place with ease. She was a yoga instructor and led sunset yoga classes on the beach. She'd already invited me to take a free class.

I'd left her alone a few hours at a time on her third day, and she had done well. I had still planned on closing the shop for the day, but she insisted on filling in.

"At least, by the end of the day, I'll know what I don't know. Besides," she said, picking up the binder that I'd been calling the *Tikis & Cream* Bible. "You put everything you've ever even thought about in this book- recipes, opening and closing procedures, you even created an FAQ. I've been studying it. Your shop is in good hands."

"I'm sure she's fine," Wade said. "Let her do her thing without you hanging over her. She'll call you if she needs something."

"I guess you're right. So, I'm going home to shower since *somebody* knocked me into the water."

Wade snorted, dropping an arm over my shoulder. "It was an accident. I swear!"

"Uh huh. Accident, my ass." I smiled though, mostly to myself.

My heart had nearly leapt out of my chest when he flipped my board. I was sitting on it, trying to get my balance to stand. The next thing I knew, I was heading into the water and Wade was cackling, loudly. In the next moment, he was in the water with me.

He grabbed me by the waist, pulling me up against him. I lifted my legs, wrapping them around his body, pressing myself into him. He was hard and not shy about letting me know.

We kissed and clung to each other, trying not to look like we were about to have sex right in Black Diamond Bay. If there wasn't a small group of teenagers nearby on boogie boards, Wade would have been introduced to the "Sex in the Bay" club.

"Why don't you come by around seven? The grill will be warm and we can set this birthday off right."

"Sounds good. Sounds really good."

He leaned over to peck me on the cheek, but I moved my head so he caught the edge of my mouth. And since he was there, he leaned a little further for a full kiss. "I got somethin' else good for you. Come ready."

"Ooooop!" I squealed as he hugged me, then hung a right toward his house. "I'll be ready," I called out to him. "*You* be ready."

"I'm always ready," he called back. "I stay ready so I don't have to get ready."

"Yeah, I saw some of that stay ready earlier," I said, laughing as I reached my driveway. In my bag, my cell phone buzzed. I pulled it out and glanced at the display.

I waved to Wade, then climbed the front porch steps and picked up the call. "Hey Paige!"

"What up birthday girl! I've been trying to call you all day! Where have you been?"

"Oh, I... had plans."

"You... had plans?"

"Yeah. I... had plans."

I unlocked my front door and stepped into the house, rolling my eyes at myself. Paige would never be satisfied with the morsel of information I'd just given her. Granted, I did it on purpose so she would ask and I wouldn't have to call her to brag that I'd just spent my birthday with Wade Marshall.

And was about to spend the evening with him.

I hadn't told anyone about Wade, including Paige. He

was a fun, temporary thing, not something that could or would last. I didn't want to get anyone's hopes up.

Including mine.

But today, I was happy. Paige could keep a secret better than anyone. And I was *dying* to tell someone about Beach Thing.

"So... these plans you had that kept you away from your phone all day. Share them with me. And don't skip any details." Her voice lowered considerably, taking on a conspiratorial tone. "Especially if they have to do with *tall, dark and fuck me* down the street."

"Well...." I paused, dragging out the explanation, waiting for the screech in my ear that came a moment later. "Okay, okay! It's not what you think." I tossed my backpack on a chair at the dining room table. "Yet."

"Girl! You are so lucky you're far away right now or I'd come over to your apartment and mess you up! You'd better start talking."

So, I started talking. I carried the phone into my bedroom, putting Paige on speaker while rifling through my closet for something cute to wear. I told her about my conversations with Wade after our not-so-friendly first meeting; about his regular visits to Tikis & Creme and my visits to the house and the night we'd jumped into this fling and see what happens.

"And so you've been fucking Wade Marshall for like... how long?"

"Like... a couple of weeks. Maybe a little more."

"Weeks! And your fingers weren't itching to dial up your girl Paige and share in the good news."

"Like said, it's new. And it's not a huge deal."

"To *you*. It's not a big deal to you, Miss Dating a Famous

Producer. Who's best friend is the sexiest dude in the game right now."

"We're not dating. This is just a casual summer thing. Something to pass the time. It's just a... beach thing."

"A beach thing."

"Yes, exactly. We're having fun, not hurting anyone. It won't last past September and we both know it. The last thing either of us, but *especially* Wade needs, is any kind of controversy about it. So zip those lips the way I know you can."

"Alright. I'll keep this secret like I kept the last one. But I better get regular reports. On *everything*."

My eyebrows lifted. "Oh, you think I'm sharing *everything*, huh?"

"Every. Thing. Don't hold out on me. You know I have nothing going on since taking this new job. These jokers think I'm a miracle worker or something."

We chatted for a few minutes about her job as a legal assistant to two very demanding personal injury attorney partners. Business was booming and Paige had replaced an inefficient assistant. Learning that she knew how to do everything they needed and more seemed to have opened a Pandora's Box.

"Well, look at the bright side," I said pulling my still damp tank top over my head, followed by my swimsuit top in the same state. "The more hours you work now, the closer you get to building up enough vacation hours to come out here."

"Believe me, that's one of the few silver linings. Maybe I can come out for Thanksgiving, provided I'm not on the phone with some hump trying to fake a neck injury."

"Oh, no. You're not giving up your Thanksgiving for

personal injury fraud. You're welcome to come out if you can swing it."

"You're not coming home for Thanksgiving?"

I scoffed, peeling my shorts and panties from my hips and turning on the shower. "As of right now, no. My parents are still being cold to me. Andrew and Liam will miss me, I'm sure—"

"And, hello? Me?"

"And you. I don't want to deal with it. I want peace and quiet in my new home. I know people come out here for the holiday and I'd like to stay open. I have a couple of chai tea recipes I want to try, anyway."

"Well, I admire you for making your dream happen. I'll support you however I can. So long as I get the details."

"Thanks, P. I appreciate it. I miss having you down the hall from me."

"I know. I miss it, too. Your apartment is still vacant."

This information gave me pause. I'd been led to believe that there was a waiting list for my apartment. An efficiency with brand new appliances and a window seat in a secure building was hard to come by. "That's amazing. It's so cute and well priced."

"And still vacant."

"You said that."

"I'm just saying. If you ever want to come home—"

"Paige…" I sighed, closing the door to the bathroom to keep the steam in. "I have a date with a very handsome, very sexy, very well endowed man. I need to get in the shower and take care of my situation. Can we pick up the guilt trip tomorrow?"

"Yes, yes. Sorry. Fine. No guilt trip. Happy birthday, I love you, have fun."

"Thank you."

"Wait, very well endowed? How...uh, *endowed* is Gage, you think?"

"I don't know why you think I would know that, but I'm guessing...bullet in your ass. That endowed. Gotta go, love you, buh bye."

10

*W*ade

I had everything all set up outside on the deck. The grill was warm and holding a cast-iron skillet with the steaks and scallops I had made and the steamer for the freshly cut green beans was on standby. I'd also grabbed a nice white wine, which was chilling in the wine fridge.

I stepped back into the house in time to hear my phone chime a familiar tone. Gage was calling, probably about the samples I'd sent him the night before.

"What up, playa?" I called into the phone as I put it on speaker. I had a few things yet to do, and I still had to change clothes, so I was going to talk and work.

"What up yaself? You workin'?"

"Not right now." I searched through the drawers in the kitchen for the candlesticks I knew I saw at some point. I found them, grabbing them and the linen napkins from their hiding place.

"Not right now? What are you doing right now? Sounds like you're looking for something... what do you need? I probably know where it is."

"Nah I'm good. I'm just... busy."

"Busy doing *what*?"

The cagier I got, the more Gage laughed. We were always wide open with each other—couldn't afford not to be, so my not coming right out with what I was doing at the moment was probably funny to him.

"I'm about to have a guest, if you just gotta know everything."

"A guest? Like, the female kind? You met somebody that quick out there?"

"Kind of. It's uh... you know, that girl from the smoothie shop? Remember the first night—"

"The one that ran her mouth, then shut right up when she realized who we were?"

"She backed off before you introduced yourself. But yeah, I've been..." I blew out a breath, puffing out my cheeks. "We've been hanging out. Or whatever."

"Huh. The smoothie shop girl. I mean..." Gage sucked his teeth. I could just see him brushing a hand over his signature waves, then pulling at his goatee. "She's fine and everything but you think it's a good idea to be like... dating?"

"Not dating. We're just hanging out. Seeing each other. It's just a beach thing for right now."

"Does *she* know it's just a beach thing for right now?"

"Yeah, man. Yeah. She's cool with it."

We'd both made sure we were clear about the details of our "relationship". Neither of us were looking for anything long term or long distance. I lived in Brooklyn. She lived out in Black Diamond Bay. Having someone out here to visit every once in awhile was nice, but I had no plans on making regular visits to this town.

"I hear you now. I don't want to hear you later, talking

about how she misses you and she wants you to move out there."

I rolled my eyes, stepping back outside and setting up the candles, laying out the napkins. "It's not like that. It's not gonna be like that. Yo, what do you want, man? I've got a lot going on here and I need to change my clothes."

"You still think somebody cares about your dirty shirt." Gage laughed, then went on. "What do you think I want? These samples you sent last night are tight. I wanted to talk about using a couple of them. The ideas are flowing right now. I wish you were here; we could get some serious work done."

"Yeah, well. That's the whole reason I wasn't allowed to go on vacation with ya'll this year. We worked the whole time last year. Sheree is still pissed about that. And on that tip, don't get me in trouble this year either. You're supposed to be on vacation, not working."

"Sheree will be alright. She likes the paychecks." His voice rose for a few seconds when he asked, "Don't you, bae? You don't want me to work but you like that money!"

Sheree said something I couldn't understand, tinged with a thick Jamaican accent. The tone alone told me Gage better watch his step. And his mouth.

"Ay, man. Keep me outta this. Happy wife, happy life works for me, too. Which ones do you want? I can work on them later and shoot them over to you."

We talked about a few tracks he really liked. I agreed to work on drawing them out from the 20 second samples to full 2-3 minute tracks. Once he had a good idea of how the beat transitioned throughout the song, he could start writing. We would round out the sound with layers and other tricks of the trade when we were back in the New York studio.

The doorbell rang as soon as I hung up. "Shit," I muttered, glancing down at the shorts and t-shirt I'd worn earlier. I pulled open the front door and let Ameenah in.

"Hey, pretty." I greeted her with a kiss on a full, round cheek, then tipped my head to catch her lips. She hummed, then giggled, the longer the kiss lasted. She finally broke away and stepped back.

"I didn't realize we were dressing down tonight."

"We're not. I'll get you set up with something nice to drink and then I'm going to go shower and change so I'm a little more presentable."

She was elegant but casual in a thin blue and white flowered dress that flowed to her ankles. It tied around her neck and was sleeveless so she was showing off the golden tan she'd earned earlier in the day. And it had a split up the side so her shapely thigh made an appearance every other step.

I wound my fingers between hers and led her through the family room to the deck where I'd set a table for us with a perfect view of the sun on its descent.

"Oh, how pretty," she cooed, looking over every detail, from the colorful poppies in a small vase to the long white tapered candles in crystal candle holders to the blue and white bone china plates, the fancy silverware and the etched wine goblets.

"You really went all out." She grinned back at me as she took a seat in the chair I pulled out for her.

"Not saying that I wouldn't do the same if we were having dinner at my place, but none of this stuff is mine. I'm just using it to impress you."

"Well, remind me to thank Gage's wife for her amazing taste and for leaving everything here for you to impress me with."

"I'll do that. You want some wine?"

She nodded, smiling up at me, so I grabbed the wine from the fridge, popped the cork and poured her a glass. "I'm gonna go shower. You cool? Need anything?"

She waved me off, already sipping from her glass and pulling out her phone. "I'm good. Go. Go, I'm fine."

I hurried through my shower, slapped some lotion on my skin, brushed my hair and my teeth and touched up my goatee. Minutes later, I thumped down the steps to find the deck empty and the sun beginning to dip below the horizon. I whipped around, glancing into the kitchen to see if maybe she was hanging out in there, but it was empty.

"Meenah?"

"Down here," I heard from practically under the deck. I walked toward the edge and laughed. Ameenah had stretched out next to the pool one level below, looking awfully comfortable on one of the cushioned loungers. Her long fingers wrapped around the bowl of a wine goblet, lifting it to her lips.

"Stay right there," I told her, then got to work transferring our dinner from the deck to the pool. I was flexible, and for Ameenah's birthday, I was willing to do just about anything to make sure she was happy.

A few minutes later, we had moved to the patio table near the pool and I had dished up steak and scallops in a champagne butter sauce and steamed green beans.

Ameenah spread a napkin across her lap and admired her plate, her eyes sparkling. "Everything looks amazing, Wade. Thank you."

"You're welcome," I answered, shrugging a shoulder. I was already digging into my plate. "It's no big thing."

"No big thing?" She grumbled while slicing the tenderloin. "You're always making something delicious for me. I hardly return the favor by making you a smoothie every day."

"Don't forget those muffins."

"And the muffins... that I make for the shop and give you the extras."

"Still, I don't stop in just to say hi. I crave that drink. My mouth expects it around 11 o'clock and if I haven't had it by mid-afternoon, I can't stop thinking about it."

Ameenah laughed around a mouthful of green beans. "You flatter me, but I still don't think some juice and ice cream compares to surf and turf."

"It's not a contest," I mumbled, reaching across the table for her hand. She slid it into mine and I squeezed. "I like to cook. And it's nice to have someone to cook for." I glanced at her plate, which bore evidence that she was more than enjoying her dinner. She was practically inhaling it. "Who will eat."

She eyed me while spearing a slice of scallop and a few green beans. "I already told you about these glorious hips," she said, before a forkful of food disappeared into her mouth.

"And I already told you I like those glorious hips." I picked up my wineglass, enjoying a swig before returning to my plate. "For real, it must be nice working in the restaurant industry. You could probably drop in any of them and eat for free, right?"

"Something like that," she said. "I've worked in all the restaurants my family owns, in some capacity. It's more like visiting a former place of employment. I don't really hang out in our restaurants, even for a free meal. I see things that need to be done and before I know it, I've been working for six hours."

"I guess I can see that. But you must get perks out of it."

She picked up her wineglass, tossing her head from side to side. "For sure. I mean, our nicer restaurants are great for birthday parties, graduations, things like that. I get first dibs, if I want them. Paige and I turned 30 a few days apart. We had our party at Porter's Steakhouse, in a private room. You normally have to spend a couple grand to get that room."

"Porter's is nice. Real nice. I remember my mom trying to save up money for us to go there one time."

"It's a little on the high end, yeah. But you don't have to worry about that now, I bet."

"Not really, no. I take her and her friends there every year around Thanksgiving. But like I said—" I gestured to the table, our nearly empty plates and wine glasses. "I like to do for myself. No restaurant cooks for me as well as I cook for myself."

"I see. And..." She smirked from behind her glass. "I agree. And that's a lot coming from me."

"I will take that as the compliment it was meant to be." I stood and reached across the table for Ameenah's plate, stacking it on top of mine. The sun had set, putting us in shadows on the patio. She stood too, grabbing wine glasses and other dishes and following me back up the stairs, across the deck and back into the house.

"Just drop those next to the sink. I'll take care of them later."

"I'll do no such thing." She started running water in the sink. "You cooked; I'll clean up."

"No, no, no... I—"

"Is there an apron around here?" She opened and closed drawers, then walked into the pantry. She came back out wearing a black and white striped apron, tying the strings around her waist.

"Ameenah, you don't have to—"

"Go get the rest of the dishes from the deck and the patio. It won't take long to wash them up." She busied herself rinsing plates and dunking them in hot, soapy water. She glanced back at me and smiled. "Wade. The rest of the dishes?"

I gave up and went back outside.

Once Ameenah was satisfied that the dishes were washed and we cleaned the kitchen, I untied the apron from her waist and pushed her into the family room with a fresh glass of wine.

"I can't believe you washed your own birthday dishes."

She shrugged, kicking off her sandals and tucking herself into the couch, sitting sideways with a leg tucked under her. The split in her dress showed off her leg from thigh to toe. Not that I was looking.

But I totally was.

"I can't believe you cooked an amazing meal for me and wouldn't let me do my part to help clean up."

"I'm gonna have to circle back to the whole birthday thing." I settled into the couch next to her and set my wine-glass on a coaster on the coffee table. "Tell me you had a great birthday and I'll let it go."

"Mmmm," she hummed, taking a long swallow of white wine before setting her glass next to mine. "My day was perfect. I spent it in a place I love, doing something new with someone I like a lot. Then I had some good food and some really good wine."

"I'm stuck on that part where you talked about someone you like a lot."

"Oh?" Her eyebrows rose. She scooted in a little closer to me and pressed her lips to my chin. I groaned at the feeling of her lips on me. Cool from the wine. Soft. "What did you need help with?"

My arms dropped around her. I took advantage of all the skin she had on display, my hands roaming her shoulders, down her arms and the thigh was in plain view. "Just, you know. I was wondering who that was, that you liked a lot. And how that person would know it was him."

"So you're saying you need a clue?"

"I might need a clue."

"Now, uh..." She stretched up to kiss me, her lips lingering on mine a moment longer than usual. She pulled back and when I leaned in for more, she tipped her head back. "I thought you were from Queens. Ya'll got street smarts, I hear."

"Oh, we do. We do."

I cupped her chin in my hands and covered her mouth with mine. I swirled my tongue around hers, then sucked on it, gently, then harder with rhythm. She relaxed against me and let a long breath escape once I released her.

"So..." She mumbled, her eyes still closed, her chin propped against mine. "What are your street smarts telling you?"

"Uh, so... I think that guy might be me. Either that or you got a couple of boyfriends out here on this island."

She laughed a hearty laugh in my face. "Not saying I *don't* have a couple of cuties out here."

"You tryna say I'm not your boyfriend?"

Her eyes popped open. Wide. "Uhm... were you trying to be? I mean... I thought..."

I pecked her on the nose and drew her in closer to me. "I'm just playing with you, Ameenah. I know what this is."

She sat up, though and scooted away a little. "Hold on, though. I know what this is, too. It's me and you having a good time. But you... were you expecting exclusivity?"

"Were you planning on not being exclusive?"

"I hadn't thought about it. But asking me to not see anyone else feels like more than we agreed to."

"I'm not asking for that."

"But you'd have a problem if I was seeing someone else out here?"

I shook my head, averting my gaze. *Where did this come from? How did we get here?*

"I didn't say that at all. That's not even what I meant. I'm not asking you to do anything you don't want to do. Including be exclusive to me. If you want to see other guys out here, I can't stop you."

She didn't respond for a few moments. Then she sighed a long, drawn out sigh. "I think wine is going to my head. I don't even know what that was about."

I laughed. I saw a couple of laugh lines show up around her mouth, which was a good sign. "Gage called earlier. Told him about me and you hanging out. He was concerned about me dating, since I'm here to work. I said we weren't dating. But... aren't we?"

She lifted a shoulder and pursed her lips. "Paige was also concerned about me dating. But her concern was more centered in *why didn't you tell me you were fucking Wade Marshall* and *how big do you think Gage's dick is*?"

I laughed so hard I choked. Ameenah stretched to grab my glass of wine and handed it to me. I sucked down a swallow or two, until the cough subsided and set my glass down again.

"So my street smarts are telling me a couple of things right now. That we like each other. That we might be upset if either of us was... hanging out with other people." I paused and caught her curious gaze. "And that your friend is real nosy and has a death wish."

She laughed. "I already told her Sheree would take care of her. She doesn't believe me."

"So, Brooklyn... what do your street smarts tell you?"

"Well, my Brooklyn smarts tell me you're right. I'd be *hot* if you were this cuddled up with someone else on this island. And that it would be sweet if I was going back to Brooklyn. But my island smarts tell me that this is for fun and this is temporary and I should reserve my feelings and protect my heart because liking you might get dangerous."

"Yeah." I nodded a few times. "I see that."

"But also that it's... kind of too late to be careful."

I nodded again. "I see that, too."

"Do you? Did your Queens street smarts tell you that?"

I laughed, looping my arm around her neck and bringing her close to me again. I dropped a kiss on her temple, then left my lips there. A beat or two passed before I had put together the words I wanted to say in my mind. I needed to be clear.

"I'm not going to pretend I don't like you. A lot. Like if you still lived in Brooklyn, I would case your front porch every week. I'm glad I met you that night when you called yourself telling me and Gage off."

She giggled, the sound muffled in my neck, where she'd buried her face.

"But I'm also not trying to hurt you. If I'm honest, I'm not trying to get in deep with you. Knowing I'm leaving in September... I don't want you to regret agreeing to be with me. So, this can go as fast or as slow as you want or need it to go. I'm only concerned about you and how you're gonna make it out here once I'm gone."

Ameenah laughed.

"What? I'm having a big impact on your life right now." She laughed harder. "Fine. We're just gonna pretend I'm not tearin' it up. I'm not knockin' the bottom out. I'm not *standing up in it*. Let's just pretend that's not happening."

She cackled, laughing so hard she had to move away. "I don't even know what *standing up in it* means!"

"I don't either. I heard some dude say it and I thought it was funny. You okay over there?" I tried not to laugh at her, a whole seat cushion away from me, wiping tears from her cheeks.

"I'm fine, just shut up for a second so I can inhale. Goddamn."

I got up while she got herself together and went into the kitchen, returning with two small bowls. I dropped down next to her and handed her one. "A peace offering."

The way her eyes lit up when she saw it was a bowl of blueberry crisp ice cream made my night. I couldn't even eat my ice cream because I was watching her eat, listening to her humming and moaning, practically licking the spoon clean between bites.

"You really like ice cream, huh?"

"Mm mm," she moaned, scraping the last of what was able to melt from the bottom of the bowl. "I do. Always have. It's so... cold and sweet." She sighed, leaning forward to set her bowl on the coffee table.

"I'm a little jealous of that spoon. You gave it a real good licking."

Ameenah's eyebrows rose while her eyes slid closed. "Are... you saying I don't lick you good? Is this what you're telling me?"

"I'm not—" I didn't get a chance to finish my sentence before she pounced. My poor melted bowl of ice cream ended up back on the table and Ameenah was on her knees between my legs. She reached up behind her neck and undid the tie that kept her dress up and on her body. When it was undone, the top of the dress fell, revealing her bare breasts and hard, erect nipples.

"Ameenah, I didn't mean—"

"Hush," she hissed, unbuckling my belt, then pulling open the button enclosure to my shorts. I watched her hands yank down my zipper and open the shorts wide. Even *my* eyes got big when I saw how long and hard I was pressed against the thin fabric of my boxers.

But not for long, because Ameenah grabbed the elastic waistband and pulled me out, then stroked up one side of the taut, smooth muscle and down the other.

"Gonna tell me I don't lick good. I'll show you who can lick something."

"I... I didn't mean.."

"Told you to hush," she said, before I was inside her mouth, a mix of cool from the ice cream and warm from... well, *her*. She worked me like a piston, up and down and up and down, then her tongue swirled around my head a few times. Then she went back to licking and sucking and making... so many sexy sounds.

I relaxed, opening my legs wider, giving her more room to work. Her eyes flicked up at me while she had her tongue out, one hand in a tight grip around me. The visual caused a hitch in my breath. So did her wandering fingers, cupping, massaging, lightly scratching.

"How'm I doing? Is this licking more in line with what you were hoping for?"

"Oh, my...*God*..." My eyes wouldn't stay open and my heart was racing. "Yeah, you're licking it real good. I don't even remember what you did to that spoon, now."

"Hmmm, good." She took me into her mouth, just the tip and gave it a hard suck, then pulled me out of her mouth with a pop. "Don't want you feeling neglected or anything. Like I suck on a spoon better than I suck on you."

"Nah, babe. I'm... yeah, I'm seeing the clear picture now."

"You getting it? Good. You want me to finish? Or..."

I reached for her, but she swatted my hands away. "Hang on a minute. Let me just..." She stood up for a second and let the dress fall to the ground. She tucked her thumbs into the waistband of her panties, but I stopped her.

"No, no, wait. I have plans for those." I sat up and grabbed her under her arms, pulling her onto my lap. She straddled me without much effort....which let me see her pretty blue panties with the wet spot that made me drool.

In all of my years as some kind of... sex symbol, I guess you'd call it, I'd met a lot of women and done a lot of things in a lot of places. But right now, Ameenah on my lap with my dick hanging out of my pants made me feel like I was really doing something sexy and salacious with a young lady.

And I was enjoying every minute.

"What do *you* want?" She purred, resting her arms on my shoulders, bringing those lips to mine.

"To see you. And kiss you. And feel you."

My fingers went walking, from the tips of her nipples, which made her hips convulse and writhe against me; down the sides of her body and around back to the generous, round shape she'd been blessed with; up under the edge of her panties where I felt her, warm and slick and more than ready for me.

She shuddered as I stroked the length of her clit, then rubbed and gently pressed in tight circles, spreading her wetness around until my fingers were coated in her juices.

Then I slipped her panties to the side and, while holding her tongue hostage, pushed them into her.

She exhaled a shuddering breath into my mouth. Her arms tightened around my neck and she scooted up closer to me. Her hips began to rock, riding my fingers like it was a short, thick dick. One of her hands reached between us and wrapped around me, sliding up and down in rhythm to my finger fucking.

I couldn't kiss her *and* tease her *and* get a hand job at the same time. I released her lips, which seemed a relief to her, since her head dropped to my shoulder and her hips moved strong and steady. I couldn't keep my mouth off of her, though, so I nipped at her neck and shoulder and listened to her breathe and moan and grunt.

With my thumb, I rubbed her clit. She squealed and jerked in my lap, hissing, "*shhiiiiiitttt*" and hunching against me so hard, the couch was starting to travel.

"Hold on, babe. Hang on. Just a second."

She whimpered when I pulled my fingers from her, but didn't have anything to say when I wrapped an arm around her waist and tipped her so she was lying on her back on the couch. I quickly did away with my shorts and boxers and her panties.

"Do I need a condom? I'll get one if I do."

She shook her head, her eyes barely open, chest heaving. "I have an IUD. Can I trust you?"

"With your life," I answered, moving into position. Her thighs were splayed open, her skin flushed a pretty pink. "You are beautiful, Ameenah. I'm not just saying that cause I'm about stand up in it."

A loud burst of laughter filled the room, and she reached for me. "You go right ahead and... stand up in it, then. Whatever the fuck that means."

In the next second, Ameenah was full of me, and letting me know, loudly, that she was enjoying it. If I was being honest, I wasn't having such a bad time either. She hooked her legs around me and squeezed, pulling me closer to her. Her hips moved in rhythm to mine, sexy little grunts of *yeah, yeah, right there, right there* right in my ear driving me deeper, harder into her into her until her back arched and the tips of her nails dug into my skin and she cried out — maybe it was more like a strangled scream — over and over until I thought she might lose her voice.

"Don't... stop..." She heaved, writhing beneath me.

Like I could, if I wanted to. The length and depth of my strokes stayed steady until she went limp and her eyes rolled back in her head. "*Fuuuu*... goddamn, Wade. I hope that's what *standing up in it* means."

I laughed, but not for long because I was just about on the edge. "Gimme a little push, girl," I cooed softly in her ear. "Help me get over."

She grinned as widely as she could, seeing as how I had exhausted her, and tightened her thighs around me. I felt her pussy pulse, massaging me from the inside.

"Damn! Don't stop that. That's good..."

I leaned on one elbow and grabbed a breast, popping a nipple into my mouth. I bathed it with my tongue, rasping over the pert bud. She sucked in a loud breath and clenched around me. I kept licking and sucking; she kept squeezing, rolling her hips until I couldn't hold back anymore.

I plunged into her, deep. Kept it there through the pulsing and raging force of my release, through the twitching of my thigh muscles, through the way the overhead light seemed to be dimming and brightening on its own and how I could only hear out of one ear at a time.

When I was finished, I used my last breath to mutter, "Fuck, that was amazing," before I collapsed on top of her.

It was a few minutes before I could get enough air and hear and see and muster up the strength to sit up. We both glistened with sweat and were heaving deep breaths, trying to return the in-out-air-exchange to normal levels.

"Oooh weeee...." I shook my head slowly from side to side.

"Oooh wee? What?"

"Ooooh weee... Sheree is gon' get us for what we just did on her damn couch." Ameenah laughed, glancing down at the mess we'd made. "You're laughing. Children sit here, Ameenah!"

"You said they don't even use this house!"

"They don't. But tomorrow I guess I need to look into some kind of fabric cleaner."

"I'll split it with you. And I'm not taking no for an answer." She sighed, grinning up into the air. "It's... so worth it..."

11

meenah

"Bye, bye!"

Dionne waved to the twins that toddled out of the shop, each sucking on a sippy cup full of fruit smoothie, followed by their parents drinking full sized versions of the same. Wade and I stood to the side and watched them all walk out of the door and head down the sidewalk.

The couple and their adorable boy and girl had been on the island for a week, enjoying the end of a long summer break before both returned to their teaching jobs in South Carolina. This time of day, they'd be headed to story time at the library.

"I'd better be heading out, too. I'll see you later?" Wade bent to kiss me, his lips tasting faintly of orange.

"I'll come by after yoga. She's *making* me go tonight." I rolled my eyes toward the front of the room where Dionne was rinsing the blender carafe and putting away the ingredients she'd used to make the last smoothie.

"You've been saying you wanted to come to yoga since I

started here," she said, holding the handle of a plastic container. "It's been a month... it's time."

Across the front of the counter, a cooler held bins of sliced fruit. Part of what I did several times a day, that Dionne had taken over, was slicing fruit, pulling juice from the freezer, making sure I had enough protein or energy powder for those who liked a smoothie that packed more of a punch.

"I don't remember asking to be dragged there tonight."

"Is this going to turn into a catfight? Wrestling with frozen fruit? If so, I can stick around."

"Get out of here, with your perverted self." I swatted Wade on the ass and pushed him toward the door.

"Can't blame me for wanting to be entertained." He turned to drop another kiss on my lips. "I'm going, since ya'll not gonna throw down. See you in a bit."

I waved as he walked out, then stepped outside the door and watched the muscles in his back ripple under his shirt until he turned the corner, out of sight. When I walked back into the shop, Dionne's eyes were moving between me and the sharp knife she was using to slice strawberries.

"Things seem to be getting kind of serious."

"Oh, not really." I picked up some scraps from a few tables and pushed a few chairs in. "We're nowhere near serious."

"Could have fooled me," she said, sliding a handful of cut berries into its container, then capping it with the lid. "The way ya'll sat at that table—" She cut her eyes to the table Wade and I had shared for the hour he was in the shop. "And made eyes at each other and talked and laughed and held hands... basically *caked* like a couple of teenagers, *ech*. Looked serious to me."

"That's not serious, Dionne. It's just cute."

"Okay." She jammed a fist into her hip and shifted her weight to one foot. "Not serious? Where were you the night before last?"

"Uhmmm..." I rolled my eyes to the ceiling, trying to remember. "Went to a movie on the beach."

"With?"

I sighed, sagging my shoulders dramatically. "Wade."

"And last night?"

"I... was with Wade."

"And tonight, after I drag those glorious hips, as you call them, to yoga you're going straight to Wade's. Spending an awful lot of time with a man you're not serious about."

"We like each other. What's wrong with that?"

"Not a thing. Except when I mention that *somebody* is catching feelings and *somebody* does her very best to deny the thing that even that old blind man on the beach can see. You know, the old man that walks up and down the beach with a tin can and a white cane?"

I sucked my teeth and rolled my eyes, then motioned for the spray bottle and a towel. "That man isn't blind. He can see just fine. He's been putting on that act since I was a little girl. It gets him more money than just being a pitiful old man on the beach."

"Well, if he was blind, even he'd be able to see that you're falling for that man. Hard."

"If you say so, Dionne. Are we ready for the afternoon rush?"

"Mmmhmmm, change the subject if you want. Don't make it less true."

* * *

I planted my feet on my mat, hip distance apart, then moved one forward, turning one foot out. Following Dionne's direction, I raised my arms shoulder length, then slowly tilted at the waist until one hand rested comfortably on my shin.

"If you're more flexible," she guided in a smooth, low voice, "you can keep going until your hand is flat against the mat." I wasn't going to take my chances with pulling anything, so I gripped my ankle. I also wasn't putting all my mind, soul and body into the yoga pose, as Dionne had instructed. I was recalling remnants of the conversation that I had summarily cut off earlier.

Wade and I *had* been spending a lot of time together. It was to be expected when two people liked each other. Were we supposed to piecemeal our time together, knowing we only had until September to be together?

I scoffed under my breath, smoothly changing positions to lower my head to meet my knee.

So what if we spent most nights together? If I went to sleep in his arms and woke up the same way the next morning? If I kept orange flavored things at my house and he had stocked up on ice cream at his? If I looked forward to seeing him, to hearing him laugh at something silly I said, to sitting close to him while we watched movies so I could listen to him breathe and hear his heartbeat, if I anticipated the several texts a day he would send that were flirty or sexy. Or *nasty*.

So what if I just really enjoyed — *preferred* being with him?

I lost my balance, and my knees buckled. I landed on my ass and sat there, cross-legged, watching Dionne lead the class through the waning sunlight. When everyone else had finished their ending pose, pressed their palms together and bowed deeply, I stood and started shaking the sand from my mat, then rolling it up.

"How'd it go?" Dionne asked, her smile bright enough to

light up the dusky evening. I swiped some sand from her cheek and picked a few grains out of the hairs sticking up around her face.

"The class was great. I need to work on my balance. I fell over toward the end and decided I was better staying put."

Dionne laughed, tucking her mat under her arm, and walked with me to the edge of the beach. She and her boyfriend had moved to Black Diamond Isles to live out their dreams. Dionne had always wanted to teach yoga on the beach. Her boyfriend and business partner, Jason, had given Wade and I lessons on the stand up paddle.

"It might help if you clear your mind," she was saying. "You weren't fully centered. And I apologize for bringing up something that distracted you so much. It's just that…"

She glanced down, thick lashes sweeping her cheek before she brought her gaze back to me. "You look at Wade how I look at Jason. And talk about him like I talk about Jason. And I know you're aching to be away from me and go see Wade, just like I'm heading to see Jason. The difference is that I *know* I'm in love with Jason."

I swallowed. Hard. I didn't have a single word to say. I watched her walk away, her hair pulled into a low ponytail at the nape of her neck, her matching bright yellow yoga pants and tank top allowing me to track her until she turned a corner.

Only when she was out of sight did I turn the other way and walk home. And thought about what she'd said.

The only difference is that I know I'm in love with Jason.

* * *

. . .

I rang the doorbell, but it was futile since the house was vibrating with music. The door was unlocked, so I walked in, only to be consumed by a wave of thick, thumping beats accompanied by a heavy bass line and, over everything, the unmistakable cadence and tone of Gage Coleman.

and see, that's where
you got me fucked up at
and that's where you gon'
get fucked up at
if you don't take
a step back now and
realize who's on this
fuckin' track now

Wade stood in the middle of a room cluttered with sound equipment, a room I'd seen countless times before when he played music for me. He bobbed his head from front to back with his arms crossed and his weight bouncing from foot to foot in time with the beat.

His laptop sat open on the table in front of him, various wires coming from every port like it was a science experiment. A Skype window was open full screen; Gage was on the other end, listening and head nodding just as hard as Wade had been.

The music stopped as soon as I walked in behind Wade.

"Why'd you stop the track?"

"We have company," said Gage, his voice sounding over the speakers. It was eerie, like he was actually in the room with us and not talking via the internet. He tipped his head up in greeting. "Hey, Ameenah."

Wade turned, surprised to find me standing behind him. "Hey, pretty. I didn't hear the doorbell."

"I figured. But you left the door open, so I came in." I

waved in the direction of the computer. "Hi Gage. Don't let me interrupt."

"Nah, it's alright. I guess ya'll got a date or whatever."

"We can keep going," Wade protested. "I want to hear how you close it out."

Gage stroked his goatee, pulling at it, smoothing it down over and over. I saw something in his eyes, in his expression. "Tell you what... I'll send you the full track later on. You listen to it and let me know what you think. Check back tomorrow."

"You sure? I'm wide open right now, G."

"Yeah. Spend some time with your lady. I'll call you tomorrow."

The screen went black before Wade could say another word. He scoffed, rolling his eyes, and slammed down the lid to the laptop.

"Sometimes he... we're right in a zone and he just shuts down. I'm supposed to pick it up tomorrow? Same energy? Pisses me off."

"I think he didn't like me listening."

Wade crossed the room in two steps, grabbed me by the waist and pulled me to him, planting a kiss on my lips before sliding his arms around me and bringing me in for a long hug.

"He's just protective of his music. He doesn't like leaks, and he doesn't like to let people listen early. The element of surprise is important to him."

"I don't want him thinking I'm here taking up all your time. If you need the night to work—"

"Don't worry about what he's thinking. I'm doing everything he needs me to be doing. What you need to be worried about is if *you're* doing everything *I* need you to be doing."

I chuckled. "Such as?"

"Such as rolling out this dough for dinner tonight." He led me to the kitchen where a ball of dough sat on the counter.

"You made pizza dough. Like… made pizza dough."

Wade glanced at me with that *you must be crazy* look. "Hell, no. I bought it at the store. They said let it sit for an hour, then roll it out. I figured that could be your job."

I headed for the pantry where I knew Sheree kept her collection of aprons. I emerged wearing a pink one with white chef's hats all over it. "Okay. I'm rolling out pizza dough. What will you be doing while I do this?"

"Supervising."

I rolled my eyes up to his. "Try that again."

"Alright, fine." He opened the refrigerator to show me how it was stuffed with fresh picked vegetables that would become pizza toppings. "I'll be doing everything else, I guess."

* * *

Two empty plates, two bowls of half-eaten salad and two glasses holding nothing but ice and remnants of Diet Coke sat on the table in front of us. On the TV, a movie was playing, but I wasn't paying much attention.

I was sleepy, my head nodding a few times before my chin came to rest on my chest. Wade elbowed me, shaking me awake. "Looks like you're ready for your bowl of ice cream and the bed. Why don't you head upstairs and I'll bring it to you?"

I yawned loudly, stretching all of my limbs. "Actually, I going to head home. I have a couple of things I need to take care of before I get to bed."

"Oh. You want me to bring a bag, or…" Wade's voice trailed off. I knew he was expecting me to fill the silence with insistence that he come home with me. But I didn't. "Ameenah, what's up? You've been weird ever since you got here."

"What do you mean, weird? You've known me a couple of months. You don't even know me to know when I'm weird."

"I know when things have been one way and suddenly they're a different way. Are you still bothered about Gage?"

I pushed myself up from the couch and slid my feet into my sandals. "I'm not thinking about Gage. I'm just... tired. And we have been spending a lot of time together lately and maybe I just... need a minute to myself."

Wade grabbed the remote and muted the TV, then got up from the couch. "Well, let me walk you home at least."

"You know what?" I turned, pressing my palm against his chest. "I really, really appreciate it, but it's not necessary. You can see my driveway from your front door. I just..." I rose up onto my toes and gave him a dry, airy peck on the cheek. "I need to go. I'll see you later."

"Ameenah—"

"Night, Wade."

I headed for the door and slipped through it before he could protest me leaving again. One of those long, strong hugs or deep, emotional kisses would have destroyed all the resolve I'd built up.

The evening was cooler than they had been over the past few weeks. I could already feel the season beginning to change. Black Diamond didn't experience much autumn or winter, but we did get cooler temps in the mornings and evenings, making for cozy nights in front of the fire. Or at Adele's on the patio, having coffee or tea and a chocolate scone.

The chill in the air meant a lot more than the change of

seasons. It also meant I was that much closer to having to say goodbye to Wade and... I wasn't ready. I didn't have to be for a while which was good.

Because I wasn't ready.

I'd considered Dionne's point of view. In truth, I couldn't get her point of view out of my mind. Despite trying hard to have fun and enjoy this "Beach Thing", I was... *maybe...* falling for Wade.

We'd had this conversation, though. There was no pot of gold at the end of this rainbow. When things ended... it ended.

I reached my driveway and turned around to see if Wade was still standing there watching me. He lifted a hand, and when I waved back, he went inside and shut the front door.

I did the same, locking the door behind me and exhaling into the still, quiet air.

You're in trouble, girl.

12

*W*ade

If I wasn't on the phone, my workout would have been easier. I liked to show up about an hour before SoulCycle class and get in a little time on the machines. It warmed me up and the weight sets were better than whatever discount set Gage had put in that puny excuse for a weight room.

Since Gage was getting harder to reach these days, I picked up the call when the music from my upbeat playlist faded out and his ringtone chimed in.

"Are you alone?" He'd asked as soon as I picked up. I stared at the phone like he had spoken in Chinese.

"Am I alone? What do you mean, am I alone?"

"Just what I said. Is Ameenah there?"

I huffed a frustrated breath and set down the dumb-bell I'd been working with. "You know she works early hours. She's *been* at work. I'm at the gym. What's your problem?"

"I didn't want her hearing the new stuff yet. You know how I am."

"Yeah, I know how you are. You like to work. I could have had her hang out in another room while we finished."

"I wasn't into how she just walked up in the house. Like she's used to being there."

"She *is* used to being there. We spend a lot of time together. Is that a problem?"

"I mean…" He heaved a sigh that was so heavy I felt its weight on the line. "I didn't call to get on you."

"But you're doing it, anyway. You got shit to say, may as well come on with it. Stop hinting around and say that shit with your chest."

"Man, I just…" He sighed. "I lent you the house so you could concentrate, you know? So you could work, not so you—"

"And I'm *working*," I growled, turning toward the wall and trying real hard to keep my voice low. "You keep talking about me needing to work, but I'm not holding up shit right now. You got samples, and you got full tracks. You just need to write, then we lay out what we want to record when we're back in the city. What about that is *not working*?"

"Nothin'. I mean, yeah, you're working. But in the down time…you know, you're just… different."

"You're in my ass right now because I'm different in the downtime? What does that even mean? How?"

"Different, man. You don't let women in like you've let her in. Seems like every time I call you, she's over at the house. Or you're at her house. You left the door open so she could just walk in, like that's her house to walk into. *That's not you.* You don't live that *"I made room for your toothbrush"* life. You're Mr. Cold Shoulder. Mr. I Got An Early Meeting. Mr. You Ain't Gotta Go Home But You Gotta Get Out My House."

Gage's low chuckle surprised me. I wanted to laugh too,

but I wasn't really into what he was saying. Ameenah definitely had a toothbrush at the house. And I had one at hers.

"I'm not saying I'm not happy to see you with somebody..."

"You're just not happy that that person is Ameenah."

"It's not Ameenah, man. Just... like I said, we live and work in New York. You got her real used to you right now but your schedule is crazy different when you're home. This vacation thing is cool and all but what if we get back to Brooklyn and you start mooning about her and work starts falling off again? She starts calling, talking about how she misses you. We can't afford that kind of distraction. You gonna run back to Black Diamond every time you can't make beats? Have her work out the kinks?"

I paced in front of the rack of dumbbells, shaking with the restraint it took to not to grab a 25 lb weight and chuck it through a window.

"What's happening between me and Ameenah is *between me and Ameenah*. None of this is any of your business and as much I don't wanna unload on you, as much as you're my dude and everything, you're treading real shallow water right now, G. And you need to take a step back."

"Because I don't have nice words about you getting involved with somebody you don't need to be messing with? You *sure* y'all are just fuckin' till the end of summer? From the bass in your voice, sounds like more than that. We've known each other a long time... too long to not be real with each other. Am I right?"

"Yeah. We're real, but we've always had respect at the very least. I don't give you advice on how to handle Sheree. You don't get involved in the women I sleep with. You never had shit to say before, so let's just keep that streak going. Keep your mouth off of me and Ameenah. Aight?"

I didn't wait for him to answer. Just like he hung up on me the night before, I disconnected the call and then turned off my phone.

I checked my watch and glanced toward the room where Roderick taught his class. First Ameenah, now Gage. Everybody was on my last nerve. It was just about time to work off some frustration.

* * *

I wasn't going to the shop. I'd decided. After SoulCycle, that I would go straight home. Have a Pellegrino. Maybe something stronger, even though it was the middle of the day. Fuck it, I was kind of on vacation. Cue up some tunes and get some work done, since Gage was so worried about it. Let Ameenah have the space she seemed to need and hope she came around.

Old habits died hard, though. I looked up to find myself standing in the doorway of *Tikis & Cream*, watching Dionne and Ameenah serve the last of their lunch rush. I took up my usual seat and waited for the small crowd to clear, as always mesmerized by the efficiency of the behind the counter operations.

Over time, I had come to understand that everything about *Tikis and Cream*, from the color scheme to the interior design to the workflow engineering, had been Ameenah's doing. She'd dreamt it all up, drawn it all out, took it from a vision to a reality.

Then got up every day before sunrise to make it happen. She was a machine. An impressive machine.

Beyond her work ethic, I just liked being with her. She

found little ways to make sure I knew she thought about me, from the orange cranberry muffins to making sure something special had a ribbon of orange flavor in it. She was adventurous and upbeat, usually. Always smiling. Sexy as hell, especially those glorious hips.

Maybe Gage was right. I was different with her. Because *she* was different. A nice change of pace and a breath of fresh air from the women I met in New York, the ones that recognized me from a block away and turned on the charm. The ones who were always willing to take the paltry table scraps I offered them, thinking it would endear them to me and... well, frankly they made me sick.

So if I liked to spend my time out here on this island — while I was *working* — with a genuine woman who was real from tip to toe... what difference did it make? What did it matter to him?

I leaned forward, folding my arms on the table. Then tipped even more and rested my forehead on my arms. The more I thought about it, I knew full well what difference it made and what it mattered to Gage. He saw what I was doing gymnastics to not see.

I was on my way to falling in love with her.

"Hey..." Ameenah's touch sent a shiver through me. "Are you not feeling well?"

I sat up at the sound of her voice. Her eyes were round with concern, her mouth turned down at the corners. A wrinkle of worry made a divot in her forehead.

"Nah," I said, twisting my body so I sat sideways in the chair, inviting her to step between my legs. Her smile was cautious and wary, but she moved in until she was close enough to kiss. "I'm good. How are you feeling today?" I asked her, hoping she caught my drift.

"I'm okay." She drew her lips in and averted her gaze.

I grabbed her hands and held them, squeezed the cold tips of her fingers between my palms. "Just okay? You're usually doing better than that." She shrugged, opened her mouth to say something, but closed it again. "Ameenah, you can talk to me. Is there something I should know?"

"No." She shook her head, her curls waving along with it. "Nope, I'm okay. I... my schedule is starting to catch up to me, I think Last night, I was just overtired. Early mornings and late nights and a lot of... *activity*."

She smiled then and winked at me. I wanted to feel encouraged by that, so I chose to be.

"Okay. So, you're saying what? You need a timeout?"

"I don't *want* a timeout, necessarily. I don't know what I'm saying. I'm just...I'm...weird, and maybe that's why. Maybe I'm tired, maybe I'm used to being alone, maybe you and I spending so much time together is an adjustment I wasn't prepared to have to make."

"Aight, so... I mean... I don't know what to say to make this better."

"I know." She leaned forward, resting her forehead against mine. "I don't either. Slowing down means not seeing you as much. But we don't have a lot of time together so I don't want to..." She sighed, her shoulders sagging.

I placed my hands on those shoulders and gave her a light squeeze. Then slid them down to her elbows and transitioned to her hips and squeezed those, too. Her arms lifted, then closed around my neck. I kissed her, light and sweet. Not at all like I wanted to kiss her, but I felt like more might overwhelm her and that was the last thing I wanted to do to her at the moment.

"Look... I have some things going on. You know, with the music. I could use a little more time to work while I'm out here. I'm not saying we take a break or a timeout or anything, just... you know what I'm saying?"

"We don't have to spend every waking moment together."

"Right. Not that I don't want to..."

"Same." She sighed, closing her eyes. Her mouth was a tight line across her face. She wasn't happy. Neither was I. But a step back would be good for both of us. "But we should maybe... chill for a minute."

"Yeah. But I'm still gonna come in for my Frozen Sunshines. If that's cool."

She faked a light-hearted laugh really well, pulling away, stepping back and busying herself around the shop. It felt like that moment when the sun goes behind a cloud — immediate coolness, loss of brightness and warmth. I already missed her, and she was standing right in front of me.

"It's cool. Like I said the night we met, I will happily take your money." She turned to Dionne and asked her to make my Frozen Sunshine. I watched and waited, paid for my drink, but when it came, all frothy with a dollop of whipped cream, I didn't really want it.

I only wanted it when Ameenah was making it for me.

I took it anyway, sucking down the sweet orange blend as I walked out of the shop, waving to her as I left. I didn't feel good about that conversation at all. I wished I'd kept my original plan of not going in there, not talking to her, giving her space without having to talk about giving her space. Now I was gonna be stuck for a few more weeks in a big ass — *too* big ass— beach house, thinking about somebody I was trying not to fall in love with.

meenah

Three days.

That wasn't how long it had taken to miss him. That had happened almost right away.

Three days was how long it had been since I'd seen Wade's shadow in my doorway, either at the shop or my house.

We'd talked and texted, hinted at making plans for the weekend, but for the most part he was keeping his distance, which had to be hard since he could see my front door from his.

I'd spent the time trying to stay busy and upbeat. With the school year fast approaching, a lot of families were on a last ditch vacation to the island. The weather was perfect—clear blue skies, high and warm sun, the occasional breeze winding through. The beach was packed and so was the sidewalk that that wound past the shop, bringing me a steady stream of customers all day.

After work, I was making a habit of taking Dionne's Sunset Beach Yoga class. I wasn't all about yoga or anything but trying not to fall on my ass kept my mind occupied and that kept me from thinking about Wade.

Or missing Wade.

Or wondering just what the hell I was doing with Wade.

Or wondering just why the hell I *wasn't* doing things with Wade.

So what, if I had feelings for him? He clearly liked me, but that was about it. My mind wandered back to our conversation about settling down like his friend Gage. He'd said it wasn't a goal for him— *not on my radar,* were his exact words. He wasn't the type, he'd insinuated, to be looking for something meaningful.

I'd told myself I could handle the Beach Thing. We'd just have fun together. I'd have someone to share the island with. And my bed with. Then I let myself mess around and feel something for him.

"So let me get this straight..."

Dionne pushed her mug of cocoa to the side so she could focus on the enormous cinnamon bun she'd ordered at Adele's.

I sat across from her, sipping on a chai tea latte and picking at a slice of caramel swirl coffee cake. It was a cool evening and Marcel, the owner had turned on the gas fireplace. Over Dionne's shoulder, the flames danced, sending flickers and shadows up onto the ceiling.

"You meet this guy, you like this guy, you're almost ready to admit you love this guy... and then you let this guy go?"

"I didn't let him go, Dionne. We didn't break up. We're...

slowing down. And if you think about it, it's the right thing to do."

"On what planet?" She nearly screeched, her mouth full of sugar-laden dough. She reached for her cocoa and washed it down before continuing her tirade. "You're going to sit at home and pretend you don't care about him, just to save face?"

"He leaves for New York in a couple of weeks. What kind of dummy do I look like, pining for a man I probably won't ever see again?"

"You are so defeatist. You do know how airplanes work, don't you? You get on them, and they take you to New York once a month. Or they bring him here. And phones do this thing where they ring and you're instantly connected to someone you love."

"Dionne..."

I laid my fork on my plate, next to the half-eaten slice of coffee cake. Not that it wasn't delicious, but the slice had been huge and... lately I just wasn't very hungry. I hadn't had my nightly bowl of ice cream in days.

"Wade and I... we talked, early on. Neither of us are interested in a long distance thing. I'm only moving back to Brooklyn if *Tikis & Cream* goes under, and we hope that never happens, right? And he's obviously not moving to Black Diamond Isles. He lives in New York, he works in New York. And besides..."

Staring into my mug of chai, I gulped back the tear that wanted to escape the corner of my eye and slide down my cheek; tamped down the emotion that made my throat close up.

"He's... different in New York. He's famous, there. Everyone knows him, knows his face and his work. He has a legion of women to take my place. This was really only supposed to be for fun. It was never meant to mean enough to spend money on airline tickets and long distance phone service."

I inhaled deeply, then sighed the long breath out. I tried to feel like a weight had lifted from my shoulders but... I didn't feel that, quite yet.

"Well, I am a romantic, so if you don't mind, I'm going to hold out hope." She lifted the large white mug to her lips and sipped her cocoa, her expressive brown eyes on me. "You know..." She licked her lips and settled back, tucking the mug close to her chest. "Right before Jason and I moved here, we had this same sort of conversation."

"Yeah? Who was moving and who was staying behind?"

"I was moving. Jason wanted to wait another year, save some more money. I thought he was just stalling so I told him he could stay behind in Austin. Work for a year, save money to open his business. And that was the plan for awhile."

"But you two are here together, so... what happened?"

She shrugged, then offered a small but smug grin. "Love conquered all, I like to say."

"What the hell does that mean, Dionne?"

"We loved each other too much to be apart. He loved me too much to let me come out here and launch a business on my own. I loved him too much to leave him behind. We had a long talk, struck a compromise. Then moved out here together only three months later than our planned date."

She sat up, setting her mug onto the table and laying a hand on top of mine. "I'm just going to keep hoping that love conquers all for you and Wade. If it's meant to be, it'll happen."

I dropped Dionne off at her street and kept walking

toward mine. I was deep in thought, my heart almost hopeful at her words.

Things always had a way of working out. Maybe love *could* conquer all. Then I chuckled and shook my head, zipping up my jacket against the cool air.

As I turned onto my street, I saw a car in front of the house on the corner. Wade rushed out of the front door, turning off lights and locking things up. He rolled a suitcase behind him and didn't even glance up as he lifted it into the trunk, got into the car and drove away.

I watched from the shadow of the large wisteria in my neighbor's yard. A suitcase meant Wade was leaving.

Love conquers all, huh? That was why Wade was leaving, in a hurry, without saying so much as a word to me?

"*Bullshit*", I spit out to myself, crossing the street to my house.

 ade

I had every intention on seeing Ameenah that night. It had been three days, long enough to give her time and space to get her bearings. We'd talked a little here and there, enough to say good morning, have a good day and goodnight, but nothing meaningful, like before. No long discussions about the music industry and what makes a song a hit. No vents about the latest Black Diamond Business Council meeting, or endless pacing and brainstorming about new innovations she could bring to the shop.

It had been a long three days.

It hadn't been quiet, though. I'd been using the time to work, since Gage kept bringing up the subject. He had lent me the house to get me out of New York, to kill the distraction that the resurgence of my father brought to my life. And, to be real, I was grateful. I had no problems working on the island and I would have brushed off Gage's comments if he wasn't hell bent on blaming Ameenah for something she had nothing to do with. He wasn't a fan of exchanging one distraction for another... but *she wasn't a distraction*.

We didn't normally get into it like that and I almost didn't know how to come back from it. Our conversations had been tense, all business for a couple of days after our argument. I kept the talk focused on the work, even when Gage tried to turn it more personal. I meant what I said— Ameenah was none of his business. By this morning, though, Gage seemed to be back to normal and so I was I, for the most part.

I was trying to time when she'd be home and I could drop over to her house, see if I could clear some things up between us. I'd showered, cleaned up my goatee, brushed my hair, splashed on a little of that Jean Paul Gaultier she seemed to like and had just pulled on a pair of pants and a sleeved shirt in baby blue, her favorite color, when the cell rang out with my mom's ringtone.

I hadn't talked to her in a few days, so I picked up the call and put her on speaker while I finished getting dressed.

"Hey, Ma. What's cookin'?"

"Wade? Son, where are you?"

"I'm... what do you mean, where am I? Where've I been all summer?"

"So you're not here? In New York? Doing a show with Ruben tonight?"

My world tilted on its axis so forcefully, I lost my balance. I made it to the edge of the bed and eased my way down.

"No, Ma. I'm not in New York doing a show with Ruben. What's going on?"

I listened with horror—and rage as my mother

described being out at Canelle, a pastry and coffee shop in Jackson Heights, with a few of the Biddies and running into Ruben. Rather, he ran into them; just *happened* to show up at the same spot.

My father was, by all accounts a handsome man. Prison had served him well— three hots and a cot and a cushy "job" running the weight room had turned out a specimen. I didn't imagine that he had any trouble with the ladies. I was the spitting image of him, like he lopped of a limb and it grew into a whole another person. Anyone walking down the street seeing his face saw mine as well.

"Not ten minutes after we sat down with our orders, he walked in," Ma said. I detected a tremor in her voice that I hoped was more anger than fear. "I need my raisin danish and coffee or my day doesn't go right. Anyway, he introduced himself to the ladies. He was charming; he made nice, you know? Then he opened this folder he had with him and handed out these flyers that said he was appearing at *Tonic*, that club over near Times Square?"

I knew Tonic well. And I knew the club owner, Drae, very well. My head shook involuntarily. Drae knew better than this. Way better. My manager, Fontaine, would have never booked this show, so Ruben had gone around everybody to make this happen.

In the back of my mind, I wondered how much that cost.

"Me and Gage do a lot of shows there. He said he was gonna be there?"

"You too. Says right here on this paper... Ruben Marshall live, appearing tonight. Accompanied by legendary, award winning producer Wade Marshall."

"*Appearing*? To do what?"

"He didn't say. I assumed he was singing, but... maybe you were supposed to be the big show."

"But—" I huffed, leaning forward, resting my elbows on my knees. I was a little light headed. And a lot furious. "I don't understand how this even happened. I know Fontaine doesn't know about this, or he would have called me. So Ruben's gonna *appear...* and do *something...* and when I don't show, then what?"

"Then he probably says you flaked or something came up."

"Leaving him on that stage looking like a dummy, with my name attached to his. Which reflects back on me. And on Gage and on our whole crew. Man!"

I stood, exhaling heavy breaths, heading toward the closet. "Ma, listen. I'm about to see if I can get on a flight out of here. If you hear from him, don't say nothin'. You hear me? I don't need him knowing I'm coming to bust up his little coming out party."

"Shouldn't you call Tonic and—"

"I'll deal with Tonic. Me and the manager go way back. I can't believe he didn't call me to confirm this shit show. Could have shut it way down, right out of the gate."

"Son, calm down. There's no reason you have to fly all the way up here just to deal with him tonight. You might not even make it before he's supposed to start. Why not just let him fall on his face?"

"Because he's using my name, Ma! He's trying to get over, using my name, my connections, my reputation."

"But you could just call Tonic and cancel the show—"

"Nah. I want to deal with him face to face, right now, once and for all. I want him out of my life and out of yours. For good."

She sighed, probably regretting that she'd taught me to follow through on things I believed in, things I decided to do. She wouldn't be able to talk me out of it. She'd taught me that, too— stand firm in your convictions. "Be safe, son. Let me know when you've landed."

I called Gage and filled him in, then asked if he could arrange the use of a private jet. He had an account with a service that was virtually on-demand. He immediately agreed and hopped on another phone to make arrangements. When he hung up the other line, he confirmed that I could get on a Gulfstream headed for New York.

"But it's leaving in an hour or so. You gotta fly to the air strip. You want me up there, man? I'll meet you if I need to."

"I should be able to handle it. Appreciate the offer though."

"Everything aside… I'm with you if you need me to be. Say the word, I'll be right out." I chuckled and halfway grinned. This was Gage's way of apologizing.

"Thanks. If I need you, I'll send the word out. And thanks for the ride. I'll keep you in the loop of how things work out."

I hung up, thinking I should call Ameenah, but I still had to pack and the airport was an hour away. I had to move, so I threw some clothes into a small carryon, grabbed my phone and my wallet and closed up the house.

I glanced over at Ameenah's darkened house, a single light glowing on the porch as I sped by. At least she didn't see me leave.

I made it to the strip just in time to hand the porter my bag and climb the steps into the aircraft. The flight was only about half full, so eight of sixteen seats were occupied by men likely heading back to the city after a brief break with their families.

I didn't *want* to be leaving and wasn't planning on make it a long return to New York. I wanted to handle this business with Ruben and come right back to Black Diamond. I'd become accustomed to the island— the sea air, the slower pace, the sound of the bay outside the window, the view of the rolling waves and white sand from anywhere in the house.

And Ameenah... I didn't want to leave her at all. If I could figure out a way that things could work out between us, it would be worth a shot but as it was, I didn't see it. I just hoped I would get the chance to say goodbye to her before leaving the island for good.

The flight was short, a straight shot northeast. We landed at a strip outside JFK and from there I hopped right into a cab and headed into the city. I obsessively checked my watch; Ruben planned on "appearing" around ten o'clock and I was hoping to catch him— and Drae, the manager at Tonic— before things got out of hand.

"Traffic is heavy tonight," the cabbie said over his shoulder. He pointed toward the throng of cars stopped in front of Tonic, causing a backup a block long.

"If you can drop me at the corner, that would be fine."

I paid the cabbie and hopped out, then jogged with my suitcase to Tonic, opting to head to the side door instead of trying to get through the front door. I knew the bouncer, but I didn't want anyone outside to know that I was there. I did happen to see the marquee, bragging bold and bright— Ruben and Wade Marshall- LIVE- Tonight!

I shook my head, heading down the alley to the side door. I still had no idea what Ruben was planning to do aside from show up. And when he showed up without me? Then what?

I banged on the door with the usual strength and

rhythm. In a few seconds, I heard the locks slip and the door swung open, revealing the short but stocky frame of the club manager in a t-shirt and jeans. His baby locs were unkempt and his graying beard raggedy. He didn't usually get "nice looking" as he called it, until right before opening.

"Ay, man! I was wondering when you was gonna show up." He held his hand out for a shake. I gave him the usual daps, then punched my knuckles into his chest. "*Owwww*," he whined, rubbing the spot where I'd dug into him. "Fuck is wrong with you?"

"Why didn't you call me about this shit tonight, Drae?"

"Fuck you talkin' bout, this shit tonight? This was your idea."

"The hell it was," I fumed, pushing him aside. "Let's go to your office. We need to talk."

Drae trailed me to his office, a room underground, beneath the club. What it lacked in light and a welcoming atmosphere, it made up for in space and looking like the Champagne Room at your favorite stripper joint. Leather chairs, a private dance floor including the requisite brass poles, a private bar, plush carpeting and a large L-shaped desk and oversized chair, which he occupied as soon as we walked into the room.

He pulled a cigar from the humidor next to his desk and stuck one end into his mouth. "You want one? Got some nice new Cubans."

I shook my head. "No. I don't want a cigar. I want to know how you know my father and how he got you to book him a show here without going through Fontaine. With my name. Man, I haven't been around all summer. You knew I was going away."

"Yeah, I knew. But dude came in on some father-son shit, talking about how he'd been spending time with you, putting together some music. He said he'd talked to you about it, that Fontaine was cool with everything, to go ahead and book it and ya'll would be in touch."

I blinked. Hard. Incredulous, I ran a palm over my head, then scrubbed it down my face. "So you fell for that line, the father-son bullshit. Knowing my history with him, you didn't talk to anyone to confirm it was happening? Fontaine would have told you it was some made up nonsense. What's he even supposed to be doing tonight?"

"He didn't say," Drae answered. "He said you and he were still working on the set.'

"So how much did he offer you for the spot? And don't play me— I know you wouldn't do this shit if it wasn't about some money."

Drae sucked on his cigar, then blew out a plume of smoke. "Handed over five grand. Cash. Money talks, you know what I'm sayin'?"

"Fi—when have I ever offered you five grand for a spot here, Drae?" And, more to the point, where did Ruben get five grand from, a few months out of prison? He was supposed to be on parole, on his best behavior, out on work assignment. Not using my name to book clubs.

Drae leaned back in his executive leather chair and chewed on the end of his cigar. He was nowhere near as stressed as he should have been. "You know... I figured, when I hadn't heard from you to go over a set list and lighting, that you had nothing to do with this show. And when I talked to Fontaine earlier, he didn't say anything about it."

"So you're not a total idiot. You know the show is bogus, so why is my name still in lights on the front of your building?"

"Because your name draws a crowd," he answered, his wide smile full of missing teeth. "I figured he'd get up there

— if he even showed up— do a little something, then we'd say you couldn't make it but stay and enjoy the drink specials. I booked a DJ to spin, so we would have been fine."

"But everyone would be thinking I was a flake for not showing up tonight."

He shrugged, poking the cigar between his teeth. "Not my problem."

I bit down on my tongue to avoid saying something I might regret.

But I couldn't help it. "We are supposed to be partners, Drae. You scratch my back, I scratch yours. I got a new record coming out, I premiere it at your club. You're talking about how my name draws a crowd— you can't even get on this block tonight. You, me and Gage go way back. We've known each other a long time and that's supposed to mean I can trust you.

"But if I can't trust you to protect my name and my business, there's no need to keep booking this club for gigs. You and I both know Gage could do the 40/40 Club but he chooses to perform here because of our relationship."

I stalked toward the door, hoping to get through it before I ripped it off of its hinges. "Nice to know that relationship sold for five grand."

Drae said something to me as I walked out of the door but I wasn't listening. I stomped through the underground level and up the stairs to the club level, nodding at a few people I knew, offering a fist bump to those passing by. I made my way to the sound booth, where Obie, the DJ was beginning his set up.

"What up, Obie?" We exchanged the usual daps, then clasped hands and did the manly, half hug thing.

"It's all good, Wade. Thought you was on summer vaca. Some island somewhere."

"I'm still resting. Had to come into town to deal with some things. What have you heard about this show tonight?" I leaned up against a pillar, admiring the new state-of-the-art sound console he was using.

"Just that he's your pops and one of you would let us know what the deal was when you arrived. Like normal."

I tensed, gritting my molars together. *Like normal.* He even knew my usual routine. To avoid leaks and surprises, no one in the club would know what we were bringing until we showed up. That was how we had always worked, and now that I thought of it, our process had been profiled in some magazine a few years ago. Ruben must have gotten a hold of it and tucked it away for future use.

"Yeah, well, I'm just saying. If I was you, I would expect to spin tonight. At least until Drae's guest DJ shows up. This guy's a fuckin' charlatan and I'm about to shut it down. I don't know him from Adam and I definitely didn't book a damn show with him. I can't even believe Drae set this up without calling me."

"No shit?" Obie stopped moving crates of records and straightened up to stare at me. "You didn't know about this?"

I shook my head. "My Ma called me this afternoon, I guess wanting to know why I didn't tell her I was back in town and doing a show with my long lost father. I hopped on a flight, didn't even land an hour ago. I was hoping to see him before he embarrassed me in front of all of New York, but—"

Just then a door opened, spilling a beam of light across the main stage. I knew from his shadow, the shape of his body and how he moved that it was Ruben.

"Excuse me," I muttered to Obie, then headed for the stairs. I made it to the floor just as he was making his way to the booth.

"Oh..." The look of surprise on his face was mildly satisfying. He hadn't expected to see me. He'd planned on destroying my career without me even knowing.

"Oh," I mimicked, stepping close. "You didn't think you would see me, did you? Didn't think my mother would call me to warn me about this bullshit you booked— and paid for. I don't pay for spots, Ruben."

"Now hold on, son. I just wanted—"

"Nuh uh. Let's cut that off right now." My brow furrowed and I shook my head, slowly back and forth, seething all over him. "My mother calls me *son*. You are no more a father to me than that dying ficus tree in the corner. You haven't earned the right to call me son."

"You wait a goddamn minute," Ruben said, straightening up nice and tall like he could even attempt to tower over me. I had a good inch and a half on him, at least. "I been up at Fishkill all those years, feeling bad about how much you hated me. I wasn't there for you because of a stupid mistake and I get that. But you are half me, half my bloodline— you look just like me, so don't stand here and tell me I'm not your father."

"And yet, here I am. Standing here telling you that you are not my father. Stupid mistake? How about a stupid mistake and then a refusal to stand up for people who were counting on you, man? You left my mother and your child high and dry on some honor shit. I might have been willing to talk to you when I got back here at the end of the summer, but this stunt tonight?"

I shook my head, frowning hard. "This takes it over the edge. There is no show tonight. I already canceled it with Drae."

"Our names are still up outside and I have—"

I grabbed the cd he produced from his pocket, slipped it out of its jewel case and crushed it in my fist.

"You. don't. have. shit," I hissed, dropping the mirrored pieces to the beat up wooden floor. "You never did. You don't get to come out of prison and act like you know me, act like we are some part of a legacy together. You are no one to me. I despise you. And so does my mother."

His mouth hung open as he stared at the pieces of the disc scattered around us. His eyes lifted to mine, a glossy sheen over the dark amber irises. "Son...Wade, I just wanted to... I thought if we..."

I stepped aside, intending to leave as soon as I said my piece. "Make this the last time I have to speak to you about using my name and my reputation. And I don't want to hear about you bothering my mother again. If I do, I'll be paying a visit to your parole officer. Because I don't know where you got five thousand dollars from, but I'm betting the source isn't legal."

I passed him, brushing his shoulder as I did so, and loped out of the room, headed back to the offices. I didn't even turn around to say the rest.

"Disappear, Ruben. I don't want to see you again. Take my advice and disappear."

15

*A*meenah

"I'm so sorry! I didn't mean to break it!"

"You didn't break it. It's sturdy. It's just..." I jiggled the lever on the new-to-me slushie machine that I had just installed the day before. I saw why a company out on St. Simon's Island, Georgia, was selling it. "It's just a little sticky."

"It's a lot sticky, Ameenah. How are we supposed to serve slushies out of this?"

I reached behind the machine and turned it off. The mechanical whirring of juice and ice in the machine slowed to a crawl, then stopped.

"You're not, today. Let's dump this stuff out of it and I'll look at it later on."

I heard the shuffling of feet at the door of the shack and turned around to greet our newest customers... but I froze as soon as I'd turned around. My jaw fell open and my mind went blank.

"Uhm...hi, there." Dionne tried greeting the middle-aged couple standing in the middle of the shop, looking completely out of place in their New York summer attire. They mumbled a hello, then glanced around, looking for a table where they could sit. I only had tables along the walls and the front of the shop with the gaping, open space that showed off a view of the beach.

"Mama. Daddy, what... what are you guys doing here? Did you call? I wasn't..."

"Well," my dad started, easing into a chair. "We heard your little venture was doing alright. Hadn't really seen any pictures or... heard much from you."

He slipped a pair of keys into the pocket of bright yellow knee-length shorts. The collar of his cotton t-shirt was damp.

My mother glistened with a light sheen of sweat in a sleeveless black top and matching shorts. "We had some business in Houston, so we took a little detour. Visit our daughter. See what — " She glanced up into the rafters at the ceiling fan slowly rotating, not stirring up a breeze at all. "... this is all about."

I moved around the counter to the front of the shop. "Well, um... it's good to see you. Welcome, welcome." I hugged and kissed them both, though I wasn't feeling loving and welcoming at the moment.

I inhaled and exhaled, trying to come to grips with the fact that my parents had just *shown up* on the island, already looking down their noses at my place of business. I wanted to be proud, to show it off to them. I wanted them to see that they had taught me well, that I knew what I was doing and that it had been a great idea, a good investment of money and that I was happy.

I brightened, clapping my palms together. "So this is my shop! *Tikis & Cream* on the boardwalk. As you can see, I'm as close to the beach as I could get without having to pay for beachfront real estate. We have a nice view and I do a good bit of business."

I turned and pointed to Dionne, who stood ramrod straight in front. "This is Dionne. She works here part time so that I don't run myself into the ground. And she teaches yoga on the beach at sunset."

"Oh, you have an employee. Impressive." I skipped the comment from my father that could be read either as condescending or actual pride. Or a little of both.

"She's new to the island, too. Her boyfriend runs Recreation Rental , if you wanted to rent kayaks or a stand up paddle or a canoe—"

"I don't think we're quite canoe people, dear. But it sounds nice, I'm sure." My mother adjusted the large black purse she drags everywhere. "We are hot and tired. We booked a room at The Bay Inn, since you don't have room for us at the house."

I rolled my eyes at the jab, then let it go. "Okay, great. Why don't you go check in, relax and cool down? I close up the shop in a few hours, so I'll call you and we can meet for dinner."

"Fine," said my dad, rising and pulling the keys out of his pocket, though he wouldn't need them. The Bay Inn was less than a block away. "But I don't want any boardwalk food. Hot dogs and what not. I'd like an actual meal."

"We have nice restaurants here, Daddy. We always have. And for dessert maybe we can go to Adele's, grandma's favorite bakery. Dionne and I went there the other night—"

"Your father doesn't need anymore sweets. His sugar is already too high."

My parents ambled out of the shop, mumbling the entire way. As soon as they were gone, I turned to Dionne and gave her a withering look. Her face broke into a wide, sympathetic smile.

"I take it the folks weren't into your idea to move to an island and start a business."

"Oh you got that impression?" I walked around the perimeter of the shop, pushing in chairs and placing the menus back in their holders. "What gave it away?"

"The way they had something slick to say about everything. My parents were the same way. They haven't even come down here to see how we're making it, but it's okay. Jason and I are doing just fine, with or without their approval."

"That's the thing. I don't need them to love it but..." I huffed a breath while pulling the bag of garbage from the can, then tying the ends in a knot. "It sure would be great if they could just see things from my point of view."

"You want me to take that out?"

I shook my head, picking up the bag. "No. Actually, do you mind closing up today? I'm going to head home and clean up. They'll want to come by the house, even if they aren't staying there."

A half hour later, I was rushing from room to room putting things away, straightening things. I wasn't expecting company, and my hours meant my housekeeping skills had gone a little slack. Wade had left a few things around and I wanted to be sure to grab them up and put them away before my parents saw them. They were old school and would never approve of the Beach Thing.

Not that I *needed* to them to approve, but I didn't want to hear my mother's mouth or see that lipstick covered frown that came with an ear full of judgement. "Proper young ladies shouldn't..."

Well, *Ameenah* does.

I still hadn't heard from Wade. No calls, no texts, no notes left in my mailbox. He'd gone radio silent for some reason, and while it was probably for the best, I still wished we could have at least talked.

I missed him, hearing his voice. Feeling his energy around me, his hands on me. His voice in my ear, his breath on my neck, the sounds he made when we were joined...

I shook my head, trying to skip ahead to the next track. I was anxious to get to the point of not missing him, not thinking about him, not wanting to be with him.

I wasn't there yet, though.

I turned on the shower so I could get cleaned up. I'd picked a nice restaurant with a view of Black Diamond Bay. I hoped to have a pleasant dinner and somehow convince my parents I was doing the right thing, the thing I believed my grandmother wanted me to do. Why else would she leave the house — a house I'd loved to visit — to me?

As soon as the bathroom was warm and steamy, I stepped into the shower. Wade's bottle of Bevel *Man Cave* shower gel was nestled into the corner behind the shampoo. I grabbed it and flipped the top up, squeezing it just so I could sniff the scent. The vanilla and tea tree oil fragrance was so... *him* that it brought tears to my eyes.

I blinked them back, tucking the bottle behind the others on my shower rack. I picked up the shower gel, squeezed some on a bath puff and lathered up, letting my mind wander.

It landed on Wade and the last shower we'd taken together.

I soaped up, letting the suds cascade south, remembering how Wade liked to rub the gel between his palms and use his hands to scrub my body, stopping at various spots like the tips of my nipples and the now famous glorious hips and the warm space between my thighs.

My hands began tracing the same paths in the same way, imagining that they were Wade's. The gritty, guttural sounds from my throat bouncing off of the bathroom tile were reminiscent of how they'd sounded when I was with him, except I missed the baritone of his voice alongside mine.

Slick with soap and hot water, my fingers slipped around my engorged clit while my mind played along. I teased myself to the very edge... and then let myself fall over, with Wade in the starring role, his skin plastered against mine, his groans of pleasure in my ear while I came down.

And then I opened my eyes. And remembered that I was alone. I exhaled slowly and rinsed off, trying to bring myself back to reality.

Maybe I could call him.

I shut off the water and stepped out of the shower, grabbing a bath sheet to dab some water off, then wrapped it around me while I padded to the bedroom.

If he wanted to talk to me, he would have called.

I told myself that was true, and continued getting dressed, pulling on a bra and pair of panties, then pulling my hair out of its ponytail and fluffing my curls around my face. The island sun had given me a nice glow, so I didn't need much but lip gloss.

He's not the only person with a working phone, I thought, slipping into a short-sleeved blue sundress. *I could call. Just to say hi.*

I slipped on a pair of sandals, pulled a sweater from the hall closet and my purse from the kitchen. My phone was tucked away in its usual place, in a pocket along the side.

As I pulled it from the pocket, I noticed that I'd missed a few texts — one from Dionne, telling me she'd closed up and the shop was fine. One from my mother letting me know that they were ready to be picked up at their hotel.

And one from Wade. I blinked a few times just in case I'd dreamt it, but there it was.

Wade M

It's been a couple days and I apologize. Had to run home for a minute, handle some business. Back tomorrow. Can I see u?

I laid a hand over my galloping heartbeat and tried to breathe. Then held the phone in both hands while my thumbs shakily typed out a message.

Tomorrow would be great, I started to send. Then I remembered my parents were in town. *Dammit!* I stomped a foot like someone could actually see my tantrum.

Tomorrow, yes — late, though. Parents decided to surprise me.

Wade M

For real? All the way from Park Slope?

Yeah. I'm thrilled, I typed, knowing he would pick up on the sarcasm.

Wade M

I'll hit you when I land. You let me know when you're free. I'll be ready.

I grinned, giggling a little. *Cause you stay ready, right?*

Wade M

That's right. :) Talk tomorrow.

I heaved an embarrassingly huge sigh of relief as I tucked the phone away and headed out the door to my car. I caught a glance of myself in the visor mirror and tried hard to wipe that look from my face — the twinkling eyes, the blushing cheeks, the smile on my lips — but it wouldn't go away.

Oh well. The folks will just think I'm thrilled to see them.

16

*W*ade

I woke up with a headache. The kind of headache that makes you reach back into your memory and try to recall what exactly you did or drank the night before that had your mouth tasting like roadkill covered in cotton balls. I remembered that I'd hung around at *Tonic* and try to salvage the evening. I'd spun a set or two, and the bottle girl serving the sound booth kept me lit most of the night.

Then I moved to VIP and kicked it with some of my friends from the neighborhood and some women who scammed their way behind the velvet ropes with low-cut dresses and very short hemlines. A few of them decided I was "theirs" and didn't leave me much time to myself, but I escaped with my dignity.

Well, *some* of my dignity. My eyes were barely open before I heard Ma stomping around the kitchen. I was laid out on her couch in last night's clothes, a thin blanket covering me.

"Yo, Ma," I croaked. "Could you step a little lighter?"

I heard her gritty chuckle, then heard her footfalls —

only slightly softer — heading in my direction. She appeared in front of me in a housedress, holding a mug and offering two white pills in her palm. I sat up, wincing, taking both and using the hot tea to wash down the aspirin.

"So when my son shows up at my door at three am stinking drunk, makes me practically carry him to the couch and put him to sleep, I'm supposed to adjust my way of life in reverence to his hangover headache?"

I gave her a look, then yawned, smacking my lips together. "Would you mind?"

She let out a *hmph* and shuffled away, back to the kitchen. "Do you think you can eat something?"

My stomach growled, letting me know I could. I needed to soak up the alcohol in my system, anyway. "What are you making?"

"Turkey sausage. Fried potatoes. Pancakes. Eggs. Some biscuits."

"Ma, you're making all of that? For me?"

"No. For the mailman."

She came around the corner again, this time bearing a wooden tray. It was laden with plates of food, silverware, salt and pepper and a glass of orange juice. She set the tray down on the table in front of me and stood, pressing her fists into her hips.

"You're not going to sit on my couch all day. I put your suitcase in the spare room. Eat and then get in the shower."

"Aight. Thanks for breakfast, Ma."

"*Mmmhmmm*," she hummed, leaving the room, her sandals flapping against the soles of her feet. That, to me, was the Sound of Ma. I knew when I heard that sound that she was up and moving, usually coming for me.

I dug into the breakfast she'd made me, realizing that I was much hungrier than I'd thought I was. I hadn't eaten since the day before and had drank on an empty stomach. I could definitely eat and did, wiping out the plates of pancakes, sausage and egg and the glass of juice in a few minutes.

I got up from the couch and folded the blanket she'd given me, then grabbed the tray and took it to the kitchen. She was seated at the island nursing some tea, her own demolished plate next to her mug, and flipping through a magazine. I rinsed the plates and the glass and put them in the dishwasher, then put the tray back in its storage spot in the pantry.

"Food was good. Thank you."

"Mmhmmm. You get enough?"

"Yeah," I said, coming around the island to drop a kiss on her cheek. "I'm full. I'm gonna go shower. What are you doing today?"

"Before you go, son..." She pulled out the seat next to her and pointed, which meant "sit". I braced myself, knowing she had questions about Ruben and wanted to know what had happened the night before.

"Ma, I know you want to get into what went on last night—"

"So spill it."

"I just don't know if I want to talk about it yet."

"You'd better find some words to say to me, young man."

I huffed a frustrated breath, rubbing a palm over my disheveled hair and the lines across my forehead. I hadn't even processed it myself — the confrontation, the order to him to disappear and to stay away from her. Why and how he thought he could build a relationship with me in that way. Why he even felt he was entitled to a relationship with me.

"Obviously, I shut the show down. The manager said Ruben paid him five grand for a booking—"

"Five thousand? Where did—"

"I don't know. But I told him I wasn't going to have another conversation about using my name. I said I didn't want to see him again, and I didn't want him bothering you. And that if I heard about it, I would make a call to his parole officer, because there's no way he came up on five thousand dollars legally."

She sighed into her mug of tea, then took a sip. And another. "To think," she said, "I risked my family for him. My mother and father knew. They saw right through the charm and the handsome face to what he really was. Dumb teenager that I was, I knew everything. I "knew" him. Thought I knew him, anyway."

"You were too close, too young, too naïve to really know him. You have to step back a minute to really get a good look. I didn't *see* him until I was... I don't know, twelve? And I heard about what he was really in prison for."

Until then, I was only told that he'd *made some mistakes* and that he was paying for them. I hadn't been told the truth, that he'd been a part of an armed robbery, that he'd been the only person arrested at the scene and had refused to give up his accomplices. I guessed that was supposed to make him some kind of hood hero, but having grown up without my father, he wasn't much of a hero to me.

Ma had forced me to keep up the monthly visits so he could see me and know me, but... he'd lost his shine. When I was fifteen, I asked to stop going. Refused to take his phone calls. Never read his letters. Ruben Marshall was no one to me, and I had no plans to make him someone any time soon.

"I wish... *almost* wish I would have been wiser. But were it not for meeting him, for silly, too-young teenage love, for risking everything for the man I thought I loved, I wouldn't have been blessed with the perfect son."

If I was the kind of man that blushed, I would have been beet red. But I was nowhere near perfect. The memories of my teen years made me shudder, the way I didn't want to know my father, but acted out because I didn't really have a father. How she made it through without killing me, I'll never know. Mrs. Coleman being willing to take me for a few days to save me from sure death probably helped a lot.

I leaned over to her so she could give me her customary peck. Then she tapped my cheek with her palm. "Go shower, we have things to do. And brush your teeth. You could knock over a horse with your breath."

"That's where I was going before you stopped me to waste time talking about Ruben."

"Don't sass me, son. You're not too big for me to turn you over my knee."

"Yes, I am," I called over my shoulder, headed toward the spare room. "But I wouldn't dare tempt you."

* * *

Between the trip to the home improvement store, installing a new water filter in her refrigerator and a long drawn out appointment at Goodyear tire, I let it slip that I had been seeing someone out on the island. I could have kicked myself the minute Ameenah's name fell from my mouth. A smug expression crossed her face, her lips pressed together in an *mmhmm, I thought so* way.

"What's that look for?" I asked back in her kitchen at the island.

"Nothing," she said. "You like her. I can tell. Ameenah, you said her name was?"

I nodded. "Yeah. Porter. Her family owns Porter's Steak-house." I sucked my teeth and gulped down more water. I was still trying to recover from my hangover. "But you know... it's... I don't know."

"You don't know what?"

"I wasn't supposed to get in deep like this. It was just supposed to be some fun."

"Sounds like it's been fun and then some. But you'll be leaving the island soon."

"That's the problem. She lives there. Full time. I live here full time. How do I make that work out?"

"Do you want it to? You haven't really been the type to settle down with one woman." I groaned, shielding my eyes from her with my hand. Lightly, she smacked my hand away. "Come on, now. You're a grown man and I know you better than you know yourself. You're not that type. Or you haven't been. What makes her different?"

I couldn't even count the ways. Everything about Ameenah was everything I wanted, everything I'd been looking for and didn't know it. Why hadn't I met her years ago? All those times we'd gone to Porter's for dinner and we had never crossed paths?

"She's just... She's got her own thing going and I like that. Her own plan, her own dreams. She's smart. Funny. Hilarious. Like... happy. And she's not waiting for me to shower her with gifts and attention. I haven't even talked to her in a couple of days and—"

"Whoa, whoa, whoa there. Stop." Ma leaned onto the counter, her hands clasped. "You like this girl — woman, but you haven't talked to her in days? Is that some new macho dating ritual? What's that about?"

I shrugged. "We... took a step back from things. We needed to slow down a little."

"For what reason?"

"For... the reason I've been saying. We don't even live in the same state. No reason to get in deep with her just to leave her—"

"Like phones don't exist? You text Gage nonstop. You Skype Gage every day, but couldn't do that with her? Email? You can't catch a flight, take a long weekend off? Gage won't let you use his jet account?"

"Ma, I just... we said we weren't going to even consider the long distance thing. Once I'm gone, I'm gone. And Gage is already funny about her — I can't see him being happy about me flying out to see her."

Her thick lips puckered in a scowl, causing a deep "V" between her brows. Her head bounced with her indignance, the pieces of her wooden earrings clanging against each other. "Who asked Gage to be happy about anything? Doesn't he have enough to handle with Sheree? That boy got to mind his own business — he's got enough of it to never have to mind yours."

I smirked, pursing my lips. "Exactly what I told him."

"Back to this girl. Have you considered that perhaps you feel more for her than... *like?*"

"Like... what?"

She frowned. I saw the threat to pop me upside my head brewing on the horizon. "I do so love it when you play dumb with me, son. It keeps me on my toes."

Just then, her cell phone rang. I let out an audible sigh of relief. Saved by the bell. Ma straightened, heading off in search of the phone in her purse. "Don't think this conversation is over."

I pulled out my phone and scrolled through missed calls and texts. Nothing from Ameenah. She was pissed or she had given up. I couldn't tell which. I opened up her contact and sent her a text. I'd planned to be back on the island the next day and asked to see her.

When I didn't get an answer right away, I locked the phone again and slid it back into my pocket. She would either answer or she wouldn't. Nothing to do but wait.

"That was Davina. Wanted to know, do I want to go to this Brazilian place she's been hearing about. You got plans for dinner?"

I sighed. "Looks like I'm taking the Biddies to dinner tonight."

She nodded, accepting the proposal she'd hinted at me to make and had no plans of refusing, then headed toward her bedroom with her cell phone. "I'll say this and then I'll get out of your business. You'd better call that girl. Or Email, text, carrier pigeon, something. You never know what might happen with her, but you don't want to ruin it by ignoring her."

The forceful closing of her bedroom door ended the conversation.

"Guess she told me," I mumbled to myself.

17

*A*meenah

"You look lovely tonight, Ameenah. You always looked pretty in blue." Mama shook the folds out of her napkin and spread it across her lap. Next to her, Daddy did the same, while ordering his second... or third bourbon of the night. "Take it easy, Russell. You're not young anymore and I'm not catering to you in the morning."

"I'll be alright, Elise," he said, perusing the leather folder that held an expansive menu. Clinks On the Bay was famous for its fresh seafood and upscale clientele since it was on the upper crust end of the island. The menu seemed to meet with my father's approval, since he didn't have anything to say about the selection or the prices.

"So how is Andrew doing with the restaurants?"

"I would think you would already know," answered Mama. "He says he speaks to you regularly."

The server appeared with a bottle of Sauvignon, pouring a glass for me and my mother. When he left, I said, "He says he's doing well. He seems busy."

Busy wasn't really the word for it. The last time I'd called

Andrew, he only had five minutes to talk because he was ten minutes late for his next meeting. But Andrew thrived off of that schedule. He loved everything about Porter Hospitality and had always dreamt of taking over once our parents retired.

With me gone, it looked like they'd have to work a little longer before that happened. My cousin Liam was taking my place, but it would be awhile before he was up to speed. I'd had a lifetime of lessons and experience. Liam, who had only worked in one of our restaurants, had a lot to learn.

"He's fine," Daddy said. "He's stressed of course. It's the busy season, but it's starting to slow down."

I nodded, remembering the height of summer at all six Porter restaurants. "For me, too. The change of the season is already in the air. After Labor Day, we see a serious decline in traffic. I'm interested to see *how* serious a decline."

My parents exchanged a glance that set me on edge. I asked about it, but the server showed up again to ask if we knew about the specials and were we ready to order? They chose seafood and pasta dishes. I ordered a grilled salmon salad and waited for him to go away.

"I feel like you two are here for a reason, not just to visit."

Daddy set aside his bourbon and rested his arms on the table, clasping his hands in front of him. His wedding band and fraternity rings gleamed in the light from the chandelier overhead. "We... of course we came to see you. Houston was too close to not swing by, but—"

"We had a meeting in Houston," Mama said, picking up the story. "We met with a couple — husband and wife, like us — that want to open a Porter Steakhouse location. They'd pay a franchise fee, the menu and decor would remain the same. Everything would be the same, but we'd have two locations. Practically bicoastal! And if that takes off, maybe we would look at opening more locations. The thing is..."

"Thing is," said Daddy, taking over. "What with already having six restaurants to manage, and without you to help out, we don't really have the time."

"And you came down here to see my shop? Hoping it was doing terribly so you could talk me into moving back to New York?"

"No, Ameenah, no." Mama's head shook back and forth but I didn't really believe her. It was just a convenient answer. "We would never hope that your business would fail. You're still a Porter. Still connected to us. We want you to do well—"

"But only if I'm working for you?"

My mother's lips were a tense, tight bow on her face. A blush crept through her light complexion and heavy layer of makeup. "I don't appreciate this backtalk, young lady. I know you're an adult, but we are your parents and we deserve respect. Pretend you believe that and fix your tone."

I exhaled a long breath. Closed my eyes. Inhaled. Exhaled. Opened my eyes. My parents were staring at me like I'd grown a second head. "Yoga meditation. It helps me... relax."

"Mmmkay," said my father, lifting his bourbon to his lips.

"So what is the proposal? I close up shop and move to Houston and open this franchise location?"

"You said yourself that you'll probably be slow after Labor Day. That coincides with the time when we would need someone in Houston working on our behalf. And wouldn't it be better for you to be making..."

Mama glanced at Daddy like she was asking for input or

permission for something. He shrugged and sucked down more of his drink. "Say... a hundred thousand a year to start. Compared to struggling to keep that little shack open all winter."

I'd taken a sip of my wine but began to choke when my mother threw out that number. *One. hundred. thousand. dollars.* I couldn't think. Or breathe. I pushed my chair back from the table, excused myself with an index finger and ran for the front door and cool, fresh air.

I paced the dimly lit parking lot, very tempted to just get in my car and drive away. It took a few minutes to get my lungs back. A few minutes longer for my brain to kick in.

My parents— my father especially— had never been fans of Black Diamond Isles. Daddy thought his mother and father were foolish, frittering money away on a house on an underdeveloped man-made island. They didn't know it like I did, hadn't watched it grow and change into the bustling corner of resort industry it had become. They still thought of Black Diamond as an empty coastal town with nothing to offer but a shack on the beach. They hadn't seen the house since I was a teenager, had no idea the upgrades and loving care that Gran had put into it.

And, just as I'd suspected, because they considered Black Diamond inferior, my parents came down to the island to try and lure me away from something I worked hard for, something they never believed I'd do. When I moved out of my apartment and packed up my car, they seemed shocked that I was leaving.

I had left. And I was living my dream. And never going back.

As soon as I was calm — not choking or shaking — I made my way back inside the restaurant and resumed my seat at the table.

"Are you alright?" Mama asked me. I nodded, spreading my napkin over my lap again. Our meals had arrived, but my grilled salmon salad didn't look appetizing at all.

"I have something to say," I announced. Mama and Daddy straightened, paying rapt attention. "I appreciate you both coming down here to check on me, and to see the shop. But it seems to me that we're at an impasse about what I want to do with my life. I want to live here. On Black Diamond Isles. Not Houston. And not New York. I want to work here, running my shop. If it fails, it fails, but it won't be for lack of trying."

"Ameenah—" my father started.

"I'm not done," I interrupted. "I'm not shutting down my *little shack* to go back to work for Porter. How much money could someone offer you two to walk away from what you've built?"

I looked from one to the other. Both dipped their heads, averting their gazes. "So why you think you can come down here and offer me money to give up my dream is beyond me. Everything you taught me about running a successful business, I've put into *Tikis & Cream*. I owe it to myself and my business to give it every effort."

I picked up my fork and speared a serving of salmon. "Now...if you'd like to enjoy a few days visiting your daughter and giving well meaning, unsolicited advice on running her new business, I'm happy to have you. If the offer was the only reason you came down here, feel free to head back home tomorrow. Either way, I'm not having this conversation again."

* * *

I had dropped Mama and Daddy at their hotel, not sure if I'd see them again before they left the island. The conversation we'd had was so much unlike the exchanges we'd had before, where they cut me off before I even got started because they didn't believe I'd go through with it.

But I had, and their weak attempt to lure me back hadn't worked.

I put the car in park, expecting that they would return to New York without another word to me, but just as Daddy was reaching for the passenger seat door handle, Mama, from the backseat, laid a hand on my shoulder.

"Ameenah," she started, her rich voice uncharacteristically low and emotional. "I don't think we realized the message we've been sending you all this time."

I unhooked my belt and turned in my seat so that I could see them both. "Even though I've been telling you all this time how you sound to me? How you shoot down all my ideas and don't want to hear anything except about how I'm taking over the business, despite what I want to do?"

"We just want the best for you," she responded. "We don't want you to have to struggle. We don't want you to make a costly, unnecessary mistake—"

"But if it's costly, it's my money, isn't it? If it's a mistake, it's mine to make isn't it?"

"It is," said Daddy, with a slow, solemn nod. "It's just that you're our baby girl. A part of us. We thought we'd be doing a good thing for you and Andrew. You've shown us... and told us tonight that we just need to let go."

"And that's hard. Really, really hard when you've been around us your whole life."

Mama sniffled a little, and I realized for the first time how difficult it must be to let one of your baby birds fly away. "We don't mean to be so pushy about the business. Of course we had plans for you, but *your* plans for you are more important. We want you to succeed. That's all we have ever wanted."

My throat closed up, nice and tight. I tried blinking away the tears that gathered in my eyes, but in the end, my emotions won over and they spilled down my cheeks. "Thank you," I choked out, reaching for Daddy with one hand, Mama with the other. I squeezed their hands, and they squeezed back. "I love you guys. I need you to believe in me, that I can do this. I need your support."

"You have it," said Daddy. "You're a good girl, Ameenah. We're proud of you. Believe it or not, we are proud of everything you've done out here."

"Well." Mama sniffled and popped open her door latch, bathing the car in the dim glow of the overhead light. "We'd better get inside. Russell had a few too many glasses of bourbon and I'm interested to see how tomorrow morning goes."

"Get off my back, woman. I'm on vacation; don't be worrying about how much bourbon I drank."

Mama huffed and climbed out of the car, then opened Daddy's door. He leaned over and brushed a kiss against my cheek. "We'll come by the shop tomorrow. I want to take a look around, see how things are running. Offer some of that unsolicited advice you talked about earlier."

I laughed through remnants of tears. Daddy got out of the car and nearly tripped on the curb. They grumbled and fussed at each other, but shuffled arm in arm toward the front door of the hotel.

When they were inside, I pulled away, still in a little bit of a shock at how the evening had gone. I pulled into my driveway in no time at all and put the car in park. I rarely drove on the island— most everything I needed was in walking distance, so I would park the car for another few weeks. I got out and locked it, then out of habit glanced toward the big house on the corner. Knowing Wade would be back to town the next day and wanted to see me filled me with anticipation. And a little confusion.

We'd slowed things down, stayed away from each other, cooled things off a bit. Was he asking to see me to officially break things off?

Or was he asking to see me because we hadn't seen each other in a few days and he missed me?

Not that it mattered what the next day would bring. The next few *weeks* would bring Wade's departure from the island. I needed to keep that in mind.

18

*W*ade

I hopped on a flight out of New York the next morning, more than ready to hit the road. As the nose of the aircraft pointed to the sky and we shot into the clouds, I felt like I was leaving the city a little lighter than I'd left the last time.

Ruben wasn't hanging over my head anymore. In fact, I was sure I would never see or hear from him again. He hadn't learned a thing from his long residency at Fishkill Correctional Facility. I didn't want to be, nor could I afford to be wrapped up in him, in his history, in whatever was in his blood that kept him doing shady things with shady people.

I'd made something of myself, picked me and Ma up out of what could have been abject poverty. I would not, could never risk that. Not for a man that risked nothing for us. I wouldn't be surprised if I heard that he was back in jail in another few months.

Besides the situation with Ruben, I'd had a good visit with my mother and a well-meaning heart to heart about Ameenah. She'd been amused by what she'd called *that look on my face* when I talked about her. I still wasn't sure what the future held for us, but I realized I wasn't going to just cut it off when I left the island for good.

Short and uneventful, the flight landed a few hours later at the airstrip. The day was perfect — sunny, not a cloud in the sky, already warm but a pleasant breeze winding through to cool things off. I got into my car and headed straight for the house to drop off my car and my bag.

And find Ameenah.

It was early afternoon, just past her usual lunch rush. I stood in the shop's door and took in the view of Dionne deep in conversation with a woman in a long yellow sundress and curly hair that reminded me of Ameenah's.

Ameenah stood alongside an older man with more salt than pepper in his dark hair, in knee-length shorts and a golf shirt, an open toolbox between them. "So when I press this lever," she was explaining to him, "the slushie mix is supposed to come out, but it's been sticking. If you press it enough times, you eventually get something, but I can't use it if it doesn't work right every time."

"Looks like this mechanism here is what's sticking. It's not catching every time. If I can get to it..." He peered into the broken down machine, his glasses slipping down his nose, and grumbled to himself.

I considered backing out before anyone saw me, but then Dionne noticed I was there and let out a short whistle to alert Ameenah, nodding her head toward me. "Mr. Handsome at two o'clock."

She turned around, her eyes wide and mouth open in surprise. She'd said her parents were in town, but I hadn't expected to see them hanging out at the shop in the middle of the afternoon.

I wasn't sure what to do, but I was happy to see her, even

happier to see the white sleeveless sundress that loosely hugged her hips. It was shorter in the front than the back so it showed off long, golden brown legs. She wore slip on sandals and had her hair tied so that her curls spilled down her back.

"Wade!"

She moved across the shop in a few steps, beaming a huge smile at me. I met her halfway, grabbing her when she was close enough and pulling her to me, winding my arms around her waist. I could admit to myself how much I'd missed her and her habit of burying her face in my neck. She wrapped her arms around me and squeezed me — extra tight — before releasing me.

"I was waiting for a phone call. Did I miss you? I don't even know where my phone is..."

"I was going to call you, but I'd rather see you. I kind of wish I would have called, though. I guess I didn't expect your parents to be hanging out with you today."

As if she'd forgotten about them, she glanced over her shoulder, made some kind of motion with her hands and turned back around when they'd occupied themselves with pretending to be busy and not eavesdropping on our conversation.

"They showed up a while ago. I taught Mama how to make a smoothie and Daddy is in fix-it mode. It's him versus the used slushie machine. I uhm..."

She stepped closer to me and lowered her voice. "It's okay if you want to run away right now. I completely understand."

"I was just hoping to make plans for later—"

"Well, no wonder she don't want to go to Houston or back to New York." The older gentleman had abandoned the machine he was attempting to fix and loped to the front of the shop. He offered a hand to me with a wide smile. "Russell Porter. Meenah's daddy, since she wasn't gonna introduce us. I heard her tell you to run."

I stepped forward and gripped his hand. "Wade Marshall. Pleasure to meet you. Ameenah has shared a lot about you two and Porter Restaurants. I'm a fan."

"I wish we could say we'd heard about you," her mother said, coming from behind the counter. "We've heard about everything *except* this handsome young man. I'm Elise Porter."

She offered me a hug instead of a handshake which I accepted. After a hearty squeeze, she stood back, her hands gripping my shoulders. "Please excuse us, Wade, but Ameenah likes to keep secrets. Do tell us about yourself— you know, the usual. Where are you from? How long have you been on the island? Do you plan to...err... stay through the fall and winter?"

"Oh, uh... well, Mrs. Porter, I—"

"So Wade has to get going. Don't you Wade? Got work to do." One eye winked at me as she stepped between me and her mother and gently pushed, walking me back toward the door. "And Daddy has to put that machine back together since ya'll are leaving tomorrow. So much to do."

"Nice meeting you, Mr. and Mrs. Porter."

"You too, son. Hope to see you again," her mother called, before Ameenah pushed me out of the door and out of sight.

I was laughing loudly by the time she'd stopped pushing. We'd ended up well past the shop, in the middle of the street. "I am so sorry about them. You'd think I hadn't dated in... well..."

"Since before Obama's second term?" I'd remembered her comment about the last time she'd been kissed.

She cocked her head and pursed her lips. "Something like that. I'm happy you stopped by though, despite my parents acting like fools."

"I'm glad I stopped by, too." I made it obvious that I was checking her out in that dress. "When do you think you can shake them?"

"We're supposed to do a sunset dinner cruise tonight. I'll come by after I drop them at their hotel. Be *ready*, if you know what I mean."

"If I know what you mean? Girl..."

I gripped those glorious hips and pulled her close to me, close enough for to feel that I was already there. Though we were out in the middle of the street, I dipped my head and lowered my mouth to hers, intending to give her one of those soft, airy kisses...but I hadn't kissed her in days and I was craving those thick, pillow soft lips.

The kiss quickly escalated to a passionate swirling of tongues and quiet moans. My hands traveled up her body until I held her head in my hands, my fingers in her hair, her body pressed up against mine. It was a moment that I didn't want to end.

But when the sound of *"woooo"* from down the block reached my ears, I knew we had an audience. Reluctantly, I broke the kiss but held her close to me. "Text me when you're on your way. I'll be waiting."

She nodded, mumbling something incoherent with kiss-swollen lips and a heavily lidded, glassy gaze. I smoothed her hair back since I'd messed it up, then ran my hands down her shoulders and arms until I held her hands in mine. I couldn't resist another quick brush of lips on hers, and then I stepped back.

That seemed to break the spell she'd been under. She blinked a few times, fanned herself with her hands, then glanced up at me with a small, sexy smile. "I need to get back. But I'll let you know when I'm on my way. Remember what I said."

"I told you, I stay ready so—"

She laughed and gently pushed me further away. "Yeah, yeah. I know the rest. I'll see you later."

And then, as if she had to force herself to do so, she turned around and walked back to the shack. Dionne and her parents were standing in the door, not even ashamed at how they'd been watching.

"Don't ya'll have something to do? Anything?"

I chuckled, waving to everyone standing in the doorway, then turned to head back to the house. I hoped I could get some work done, but if I was honest with myself, I'd mostly be thinking about seeing Ameenah later that night.

Today, I'd let her be a distraction.

19

*A*meenah

The entire day was throwing me for a loop. It had taken a few hours to get my parents to stop asking questions about Wade and talking about that fiery passionate kiss he'd given me in the middle of the street.

"Really, Mama. It's... not that serious," I'd told her for the tenth time, over a generous helping of filet mignon, shrimp and baked potatoes with a backdrop of the rosy glow of sunset on Black Diamond Bay. The dinner cruise had been amazing, full of music from my parent's era. We barely felt the movement of the sea craft as it floated along the coast.

"That kiss seemed serious to me, Ameenah." Mama glanced at me over her plate, then popped a forkful of potato into her mouth. Daddy nodded, already a drink or two into the evening. "Open your eyes, sweetheart. A man doesn't kiss a woman like that, look at her like that without meaningful intention. Do they, Russell?"

"Woman, I told you, don't get me involved in this girl talk mess," he grumbled. "But since you're asking me," he added, leaning forward a little. "The man is more than a little sweet on you."

"And if I'm not mistaken, the feeling is mutual. Mmm?"

"I... I mean. I care about him—"

"Come on, now, Meenah," Daddy said. He pierced a slice of steak and shoveled some baked potato onto his fork. "There was a lot more than care in your face today. Reminds me of when I met your mama. She had this look, see. This look that told me I was more than just some nice boy she met, that she might entertain for a minute."

"Russell, I had no such thing—"

"Please don't make it two Porter women lying at this table. You tellin' Ameenah she looks like she's in love with the boy. I'm saying I saw the same thing in you when we met."

I felt a blush crawl up from my chest and inflame my cheeks. I didn't know anything about this *look* they were talking about, but I was never so anxious for dinner to be over.

Sort of. Because for the first time in a long time, my parents and I were getting along. More than getting along... we were on our way to being close again.

After dinner the evening before, the air between us had been stiff, thick with tension and unsaid words and perhaps misunderstood motives. I was proud of myself, though. I'd stood up for myself and made it clear, once and for all and unequivocally what my life's goal and dream was about.

Now that we were back on good terms, I could breathe easier... except for the conversation I still needed to have with Wade.

Seeing him earlier today told me that my heart and my body were not in agreement with my mind. Every nerve ending from my hair to my toes crackled with heat and longing for him. I felt like it had been weeks, not days since I'd last seen him and he looked as tall, dark and handsome as the first time I'd met him.

I'd spent the day trying not to think about him, the scruff of his goatee between my thighs, his lips on me, the taste of him. But I'd seen my parents off, complete with teary goodbye and promises to return to the island soon and was headed back to my house to shower, put on something a little more... *seductive*... and see this man that had turned my world upside down when it was the last thing I really needed.

I rushed into the house and flew through my bedroom, turning on the shower and letting the bathroom steam up. It would be a quickie, no time to get myself all worked up about Wade... I'd be seeing him soon enough.

Speaking of... I pulled my phone from the bag I'd dumped on the bed and unlocked it, scrolling to *Wade M* in my VIP list.

On my way in a few. Moments later, three small dots appeared in the display window.

Wade M

Good. You want anything when you get here?

I snickered, my fingers moving across the keyboard. He knew what he was doing. And I knew that he knew what he was doing. *I already told you to be ready. I'm not gonna tell you again.*

Wade M

I meant something to drink... but I see where your head's at and I been ready for you.

Besides, you don't need to get me drunk. I'm a sure thing.

Wade M

Woman I'm just trying to be nice and offer you some-

thing to drink but you got jokes. Bring them hips over here.

I laughed out loud, updating him that I would be over there as soon as fucking possible, then tossed the phone back into the bag. I grabbed up the bag I'd been taking back and forth to Wade's house, grinning that I hadn't even emptied the stuff I usually keep in it — toothpaste, deodorant, a little perfume, condoms, a pair of flip-flops, a few pair of clean bras and undies, and a swimsuit. I threw in a pair of capris and a long tee shirt and headed to the shower, noting the pep in my step.

And the smile on my face. I didn't even roll my eyes at myself. I was in love with Wade and whatever happened between us, he would go back to New York knowing it.

A half hour later, I stood at his front door, wondering if I should knock or ring the bell or... just walk in. I tried the knob, and it gave easily, so I walked into the house.

It was dark, but not completely. A path of lit tea lights led me from the door, down the hall toward the family room. I heard music pulsing at low volume from the speaker system that ran throughout the house.

"Wade? I'm here..."

I heard shuffling a few rooms away and Wade came around the corner. As usual, he was underdressed, but I didn't mind the way his sweats hung so low on his hips that I could see the Adonis lines — the V — and the way the hem of the worn t-shirt curled up so I could see said V. He was barefoot and casual and since I had just thrown a t-shirt and leggings over my hurriedly lotioned body, I was all the way into it.

"Hey, pretty," he said, his voice so low I just barely heard it over the music. He opened his arms, and I realized I was still standing at the door, my overnight bag hanging from my fingers. I dropped it and forced my feet to move down the hall toward him.

I exhaled a deep breath as his arms closed around me. His lips brushed my forehead, then my cheek, then settled on my lips for a long moment before he stepped back, grabbing my hands. He held them behind his back as he pulled me toward the family room, where we usually hung out if we weren't on the patio. Or the bedroom.

"Hope you don't mind the sound track. I just figured out how to pipe music through the house and I liked the vibe."

"I like the vibe, too. It's nice and cozy in here."

The room was dark except for the low light of a lamp in the corner of the room and a couple of candles in crystal holders flickering on the coffee table. Two bowls sat in the middle of the table and when I saw them I smiled.

Wade led me to the couch, and we sat, settling against the plush cushions that we'd shampooed together weeks before, after our last tryst on the couch. We'd established a rule after that — no more sex on porous surfaces.

And that we wouldn't tell Sheree what we'd done on the kitchen counter.

He reached forward, grabbing a bowl and handing it to me, then picking up the other. We ate our ice cream in comfortable silence. It was chocolate cheesecake — decadent and smooth and sweet. I devoured every spoonful with moans of pleasure, knowing Wade was watching me eat it.

"You got a little chocolate on your bottom lip," he mumbled, taking my empty bowl and setting his half-eaten, abandoned bowl on the table in front of us.

"You should lick it off," I suggested. It seemed, though, that he already had that idea, since his lips were on mine before the spoon could settle in the bottom of the bowl.

When he was satisfied that my lips were free of chocolate — and lip balm, he settled us back into the couch. Janet Jackson's *The Way Love Goes* floated through the room.

"You think she's pregnant? At 50?"

"I have no idea," he said dryly, giving me a look that told me that thoughts about a pop icon's rumored pregnancy did not run through his mind.

"You don't hear the inside track on stuff like that?"

"I mean... I'm sure somebody that I know, knows somebody that knows her. But I don't pay attention to that talk. That's shit Sheree keeps up on."

"What *do* you keep up on?"

He shrugged. "I guess stuff in my line of work. Who's doing whose beats because his old producer got picked up for meth. Who's in jail, who's in rehab. Who showed up for a session so high he couldn't remember his own stage name."

My eyebrows shot up. "Damn, that's high."

"Yeah. People don't even mess with illegal shit anymore. Not when you have Doctor So and So calling you up every other week, wanting to know how you're doing, is there anything he can do for you. Get a couple of prescriptions and rotate through them. Got a friend of mine that almost died doing that shit."

"Wow. That hit close to home."

"Yeah. So long as me and Gage stay away from it, we'll be good. I keep our crew too busy to have time for that mess."

He paused, dropping an arm around my shoulder and pulling me close to him. "Speaking of my crew... I'm glad you're finally here. I had to resort to working, to pass the time."

"I'm sure Gage had no problem with that."

"He didn't have shit to say about it. He and the family were out at her parent's Yacht Club today. But me and

Gage... let's just say that we had a conversation. Gage is clear on what he's free to speak on from now on."

"I don't want to come between you and your friend. I don't want to be like the Yoko Ono of hip hop."

Wade exploded in laughter. "Yo, the Yoko Ono of hip hop?"

"Yeah. You know how folks say she tore the Beatles apart?"

Wade sucked his teeth, wagging his head. "It's not like that. Them cats, the Beatles, got together one day and made a band. Me and Gage... we go way back. We're friends first and if anything about this business threatens that, the friendship comes first."

"Okay. So long as things are good between you two."

"We're good. Gage is one of them special snowflake types — he's not used to my attention being divided. I talk a lot about Sheree but she dotes on him, and so do his parents. I just need him to respect that I know what I'm doing, that I know where my priorities are and that I am always gonna take care of him and what we do."

I chuckled to myself, but he caught the rumble against his chest. He jiggled my shoulder and glanced down at me with a raised brow as if to ask, "what?"

"I... had to tell my parents just about the same thing. They came down here... well, they said they came to visit, but..." I shook my head.

"Tried to get you to come back home? Your dad said something about New York or Houston."

"They wanted me to oversee the opening of a new Porter's Steakhouse in Houston. It'd be a franchise location, but it needs to be indoctrinated into the business. It needs to look, smell, feel, operate like a Porter Restaurant."

"You couldn't do that from here? They'd want you to relocate for that?"

"The idea was for me to pack up and move to Houston as soon as it slows down here. But not to keep me busy during the slow months... because they didn't believe that what I came here to do was important. They still wanted me to accomplish their goals. Do their bidding. Complete their plan for me."

"But you told them what was what, right?"

"Right. And then... I might have gone back on my decision to not help them set up this new restaurant."

Wade reared back, his forehead wrinkled in confusion. "You what?"

"I'm not moving to Houston. But business *will* slow down for *Tikis & Cream*, enough that I don't need two people running it every day. A lot of the shops around here let their summer help go at the end of September.

"I could shorten the hours that the shop is open, leave Dionne here to run things and fly back to New York a few days at a time. That gives my dad— or Andrew— time to go to Houston and get things set up the way they like them."

He nodded, listening intently. I wanted him to catch on to what it could mean for us. If there could be an us.

"So how long would you do this back and forth thing?"

"If they go through with signing the papers, construction would start right away, with the restaurant set to open in the Spring. Just in time for me to be back in Black Diamond full time for the busy season. But I would spend the majority of fall and winter in New York keeping the lights on."

"So... you know I live in New York, right?"

The smile I wanted to hold back made itself known, busting through my serious, slow explanation of my plan to be in New York as much as possible over the next few months. Coincidentally at the same time that Wade would be returning home.

"I heard that. Brooklyn Heights, to be exact."

"Good. So long as you know where I'll be, when you're up there."

"To be honest... I was hoping for an invitation to come see you."

"You were?" The confused look was back, his head cocked to the side. "What made you think you wouldn't get one?"

I shrugged a shoulder. "I wasn't sure how far you wanted to take this... Beach Thing. We said we would get to know each other and have a little fun."

"And we did that. Right?"

"For sure." I nodded in firm agreement. "And when the summer was over, we said—"

"About that—"

"Wait, Wade..." I shifted on the couch to face him, pressing my palms together. "Wait, before you bring down the hammer. I know you don't do the relationship thing and long distance isn't appealing to you. I really, *really* set out to just have fun with you, and it wasn't until people started telling me I looked different and I was acting different that I realized that—"

"Ameenah, I love you."

My mouth stopped moving, the words crashing and jumbling in a train wreck in my head. *Did he just say...*

"Did you hear me?" He asked, like he knew what had just rolled through my brain.

"Uh...y-yeah. I heard you. I'm just... Are — are you serious?"

"Dead ass," he replied, which, despite being completely leveled at *those three words*, made me laugh hysterically.

Over the summer, he had been teaching me all the New York lingo I seemed to have missed.

"Did you..." I stopped, because I couldn't talk and laugh at the same time. "Did you just say *dead ass*?"

"Fah sho. Nah'mean?"

I laughed harder and louder. "Okay, stop. I can't take it anymore. This is a serious moment."

"Aight. Settle down, then."

He leaned in to kiss me, which went from a brush of his lips against mine to a full-blown, sensuously erotic, emotional experience. When he released my lips and pulled back, I saw something different in his eyes. On his face. The expression stole the breath from my lungs.

"So. You don't have anything to say?"

"Oh... well..." I cleared my throat, still trying to form complete sentences in my mind. And breathe. Inhaling deeply, I sat up and moved so that I straddled his thighs. I settled my weight on him, reveling at the feel of his hands gripping my thighs, of the tips of my nipples under my t-shirt brushing his chest. "So, yeah... I have something to say. Before you interrupted me with your little declaration—"

"My little declaration? I just told you I loved you, woman."

"See, here you go interrupting me again. I was about to tell you I love you, too. Real talk."

He laughed, then grinned, his wide and sexy smile filling me with warmth. His hands started moving, making their way up under my t-shirt to cup my breasts. The pads of his thumbs scraped across my nipples, sending a tremor down my back.

"So you love me, huh?"

"Yes. And you love me."

"So... what do we want to do about it?"

I leaned in and kissed him, and then kissed him again, then pulled back just enough that I could see his eyes. "I say we dump the plan to end things at the end of the summer. And we see how far this Beach Thing can go.... if that sounds good to you."

He nodded, blinking slowly. He moved his hands down my waist, past the band of my leggings, and squeezed a generous helping of ass.

"Sounds real good to me. Know what else sounds good?"

"Well, I can't read your mind, but..." I rolled my hips, grinding against the outline of him pressed against my thigh. "I hope it involves some dick seizing and... what is it you say? Standing up in it?"

The room filled with his laughter over the sounds of Robin Thicke's *Lost Without U*.

"You wanna know something funny?"

"Yes." I kissed him, drawing my arms tighter around his neck. "What's funny?"

"So I was at home, up at this club where my father had decided he was gonna show out. I handled that and hung out for the night. I happened to ask somebody about *standing up in it* — what it really means."

He laughed again, which made me laugh. "What? What does it mean?"

"It's when you have sex standing up. "

"Oh, *pfft*." I frowned, waving him off. "That's all? We've *been* doing that. I thought it was something new."

He laughed again, then started moving, inching his way off of the couch with me still on his lap. When he got to the edge, he stood up, taking me with him. I wrapped my legs around him and let him carry me toward the staircase.

"I would be happy to do the same old shit with you,

Ameenah. Let's keep this Beach Thing going. Past September... October... forever..."

I groaned, happily. "That sounds so good to me. I love you, Wade."

His arms tightened around me, locking me in a warm, muscular embrace. "I love you too, pretty."

EPILOGUE

$\mathcal{W}$ade

I slung a messenger bag over my shoulder and nodded at the front desk receptionist as I made my way out of *Tuneage*. It was nearing Thanksgiving, and you'd think we would see a slowdown, but a lot of artists were home for the holidays and had booked studio time.

"Make sure you lock up right at five and get home. I don't want your grandma complaining about how I kept you here late. Then I gotta hear it from my mother, too."

Thea laughed, pulling the phone away from her ear. "You know Neeta don't need a reason to fuss. See you at Porter's tonight."

I took in the view on the other side of the doors and frowned. Even though it was sunny out, it was so... bleak. And it was cold as hell— brick, as we say in Brooklyn. Well, me and my crew do, anyway.

I pushed the door open and stepped into the light foot traffic going past the mid-city studio. The wind was frigid, making the low temperatures even worse. The only thing that made me feel better was knowing that in less than a day, I would be back on Black Diamond with Ameenah. It wouldn't be hot like it had been over the summer, but I was looking forward to high 70s, white sand and the sound of the Bay.

Tuneage wasn't far from my condo, so it wasn't long before I was breezing through the front doors of my building. I tipped my head at Alfred, the doorman who pressed the elevator call button as soon as I'd walked in.

"What's good, Alfred? They got you working all night?"

"Afternoon," he greeted me in return. "Just until eight. Then I'm home to help the missus. Got the boys coming home tonight."

"All the boys?"

He nodded, giving me that proud grin he always gave me when he talked about his sons. All four of them were attending Morehouse College, the oldest a senior, the youngest a freshman. "That sounds like a nice holiday, man. Enjoy that. Have you seen Ameenah come in yet?"

"About an hour ago," he said, just as the elevator arrived and the door slid open. "Have a good evening, Mr. Marshall."

I stepped into the elevator, standing back while the cube climbed to my floor. At the sixth floor, it slowed to a smooth stop, and the doors opened to a semi-private landing. There were only two condos on this floor — mine and a Pakistani couple that traveled a lot. I could tell they weren't home because the landing didn't smell like spices.

And because Rhami didn't swing the door open and yell out, "Hey Wade! You want some dinner? I made extra!"

I keyed the code to open the door to my place and hung my bag off of a hook next to the door. Ameenah's leather jacket hung in its usual spot, and her purse was on the table just inside the door. Her phone was plugged in, charging.

"Meenah?"

"Oh good, you're here."

She came from the bedroom, wearing a midnight blue dress that flared out at the waist. The bodice was decorated with sparkling, shiny gems. Her hair looked freshly washed, the way the wild curls fluffed around her face and flowed down her back.

In her hands, she held a thin silver chain that had a small diamond solitaire strung on it. "I need you to help me put this on. It keeps getting caught in my hair."

For a few moments, I stood in the hallway, taking in the sight of this woman that I never knew I was looking for but was so happy I'd found.

Her plan to do both jobs had worked out perfectly. The work back on Black Diamond was just enough to keep Dionne busy, especially with the shorter hours. With Dionne handling *Tikis & Cream*, Ameenah was free to travel. She'd been back and forth a few times already.

And when she was in New York, she stayed with me.

She'd made herself at home in my condo, and I didn't mind at all. Her toothbrush was welcome in my bathroom, her slippers on her side of the bed, her robe on a hook in the closet. No more *Mr. I Got An Early Appointment, You Gotta Go*, for me. I loved having her in my place.

"Wade?" Her eyebrows were raised, eyes wide in concern. "Can you put this on? And you need to change. Everyone will be at Porter's at seven. You know how traffic can be."

"What's this?" I took the thin chain and the small diamond from her and inspected them.

"What do you mean, what is it?" She gave me the same

look Ma gave me when I asked a stupid question. "It's the same necklace I've been wearing since you met me."

"Nah." I handed it back to her, dropping it into her palm. "This is cool for everyday but Thanksgiving with the families and the Biddies calls for something bigger."

I backtracked to my bag and dug inside for the velvet lined case I'd picked up earlier in the day. When I came back to her, still standing in the middle of the hall, her eyes were on the black case I held in my hands.

"It's not what you're thinking," I assured her, then laughed at the moment of relief that crossed her face. I wouldn't dare take *that* step without talking to her father first. Old school, but Ma would have my head if I didn't do it.

"So then... what is it?"

"A little something for you to show off to the folks and everybody. Especially Paige."

I held the box in one palm and flipped it open with the other. Inside was a gleaming black diamond pendant, surrounded by sparkling diamonds.

"Wade," she whispered behind a trembling hand covering her mouth. "It's... beautiful. And it's a black diamond."

"A memento of where we met. Where we fell in love. Where we started this never ending Beach Thing. You like it?"

She practically threw herself against me, so hard I almost dropped the box. She squeezed me tight, then plopped a kiss on my lips.

"I love it. I love *you*. Put it on?"

She turned around and lifted her hair out of the way so I could fasten it around her neck. It hung exactly the way I knew it would and looked amazing against her skin. She ran to the hallway mirror and stood on her tiptoes to get a good look at it. The way she fingered it and smiled let me know I'd made a good choice.

I stopped to kiss her cheek as I passed her on the way to the bedroom to change for dinner. Tonight would be a great night at Porter's Steakhouse, full of good food and a big, happy family.

Tomorrow, we would be back on the island for a few weeks, getting in a little beach time before the rush of the holiday season. Gage, Sheree and the kids were joining us so we could get some work done, too.

I couldn't wait to be back where it all began.

"Love you, Beach Thing."

ABOUT THE AUTHOR

For as long as she can remember, Author DL White would much rather be in her bedroom reading and writing than doing anything else, but she began seriously pursuing a writing career in 2011.

She harbors a love for coffee and brunch, especially on a patio, but her true obsession is water— lakes, rivers, oceans, waterfalls! And sand... dig your toes in, soft! On the weekend, you'll probably find her near water and if she's lucky, on an ocean beach.

By day she is an Executive Administrative Assistant. By night, when not writing books, she devours them. She blog her reviews and thoughts on writing and books at BooksbyDLWhite.com.

facebook.com/BooksbyDLWhite
twitter.com/Author_DLWhite
instagram.com/author_DLWhite

OTHER BOOKS BY THIS AUTHOR

BRUNCH AT RUBY'S

DINNER AT SAM'S, A RUBY'S NOVEL

UNEXPECTED, A HOLIDAY SHORT

LESLIE'S CURL & DYE, POTTER LAKE #1

SECOND TIME AROUND, A POTTER LAKE HOLIDAY SHORT

THE GUY NEXT DOOR, A POTTER LAKE NOVEL